Magnified 100X

The Suspicion

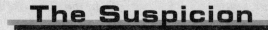

Even the book morphs!
Flip the pages
and check it out!

Look for other **ANIMORPHS**® titles by K.A. Applegate:

ANIMORPHS®

The Suspicion

K.A. Applegate

AN
APPLE
PAPERBACK

SCHOLASTIC INC.
New York Toronto London Auckland Sydney
Mexico City New Delhi Hong Kong

ISBN 0-590-76257-5

Copyright © 1998 by Katherine Applegate. All rights reserved. Published by Scholastic Inc. SCHOLASTIC, APPLE PAPERBACKS, ANIMORPHS and associated logos are trademarks and/or registered trademarks of Scholastic Inc.

12 11 10 9 8 7 6 5 4 3 2 1   8 9/9 0 1 2 3/0

Printed in the U.S.A.   40

First Scholastic printing, December 1998

For Michael and Jake

The Suspicion
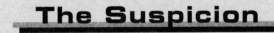

CHAPTER 1

Go forth, mighty warriors! Go forth into space! All the galaxy shall tremble before the Helmacrons. All will obey us. All will be our slaves. For only we are truly worthy to be Lords of the Universe.

— Posthumous Exhortation of the Emperor.
From the log of the Helmacron ship, *Galaxy Blaster*

My name is Cassie.

There are a lot of things about me that I can't tell you. My last name, for example. Or my address.

I live in a paranoid world. I wish I didn't, but I do. And I have no choice but to conceal, to lie, to mislead. Even while I am desperately trying to tell the truth.

You *must* know the truth. You must accept what is happening to Earth, to humanity. Because only by knowing can you fight the terrible evil that is upon us.

I am referring, of course, to the Yeerks.

Not to the Helmacrons.

The Yeerks are a parasitic species from a far-distant planet. They originate in an aquatic environment. A Yeerk pool. At some point in their evolution they moved out of the safety and sensory deprivation of the pool and evolved an ability to enter the brains of a species called Gedds.

For a long time, millennia, maybe, they were content to go that far. They did not know about space travel or technology at all. Like humans, they did not know of the existence of other species in the galaxy.

At least, that's what our Andalite friend, Ax, tells us. I'm sure it would be fascinating to study the evolution of the Yeerk species. Kind of like it must be fascinating to study cholera or typhoid.

Study with care. Because as far as humans are concerned, the Yeerks *are* a disease. They are spreading throughout our population.

They enter through the ear canal. They have the ability to thin out their bodies, displace the portions of the inner ear that are in the way, and drill into the skull. There they flatten their bodies out, sinking into the crevices on the surface of a human brain.

They tie into the brain. Like you or me accessing a computer with a keyboard. They can see all of your memories. They know all of your thoughts. All.

And they can control you utterly and completely. They move your hands. They move your feet. They aim your eyes and tilt your head and make that familiar smile everyone knows is yours alone.

We call them Controllers. The slaves of the Yeerks. The Hork-Bajir people were the Yeerks' first great alien conquest. Then they infiltrated the Taxxons. They have had skirmishes with a dozen other species. But now they are after their greatest prize: Homo sapiens.

Humans. Humans, with fingers more delicate and capable than any Taxxon or Hork-Bajir or Gedd. Humans, who could be fed almost anything, unlike the bark-eating Hork-Bajir or the eternally ravenous, cannibalistic Taxxons. Humans, who exist in numbers far greater than all those species combined.

We are the perfect host bodies. Not as dangerous as a Hork-Bajir can be, but infinitely more adaptable.

Billions of unaware, skeptical human beings. We look, to the Yeerks, like Aztec gold looked to Cortés. We could be the solution to all their problems. We could give them the sheer numbers to explode from Earth and ravage every other species in existence.

Fighting against this invasion are the Andalites. Outnumbered, outgunned, unprepared. Like firemen trying to put out a firestorm that leaps from building to building, the Andalites try to outsmart and outfight the Yeerks.

Sometimes they win. Other times . . .

The Andalites came to Earth to crush the Yeerk invasion. Instead they were destroyed. Ax, our friend Aximili-Esgarrouth-Isthill, made it to Earth and survived to join us.

His brother, Prince Elfangor, also made it to Earth. Knowing he was about to die, he gave us the ultimate prize of Andalite technology: the power to morph. The ability to touch any living animal, absorb its DNA, and then to literally become that animal.

And who is "us"? Me. My best friend, Rachel. Jake, our very cute and very fearless leader. Marco, Jake's best friend. Ax the Andalite. And Tobias.

Tobias is living the downside of morphing. See, there's a two-hour limit. If you stay in morph longer than that, you stay permanently.

Now you know. Now you see what we Animorphs are up against.

And now you see why we really didn't need a *second* alien invasion of Earth.

I mean, isn't one enough?

CHAPTER 2

O Great Emperor, the Most Wise, the Most Farseeing, we have at last found a planet ripe for conquest! It is a very large planet, filled with very large species. But the larger they are, the lower they will be brought, as they cringe and tremble before our unstoppable might!

— From the log of the Helmacron ship, *Galaxy Blaster*

"Cassie, what are you doing?"

I stood up, feeling the ache in my back. I was in the bed of my dad's pickup truck. I had just lifted a somewhat rusty bicycle up there to join the rest of the stuff we were giving away. I wiped the sweat from my forehead and looked down at Rachel.

As always, she looked like she'd just stepped off a page of *Mademoiselle* magazine. Rachel is the only person alive who could be run over by a bus, buried in a mud slide, and thrown two miles by a tornado, and somehow emerge from it with perfect clothes, perfect hair, and perfect makeup.

Sometimes I swear it's something supernatural.

Whereas I had spent the morning mucking out the stables, giving a suppository to a very annoyed Canada goose, and then collected give-away stuff for a run to Goodwill. And I looked . . . well, I looked like I'd been run over by a bus, buried in a mud slide, and thrown by a tornado.

"I'm working," I said grumpily. "Maybe you should try it sometime."

Rachel wasn't at all offended. "I just have two words for you, Cassie: Ralph. Lauren. It's one thing to wallow in dirt, but do you have to do it while wearing boys' jeans from Wal-Mart? That's why we have Ralph Lauren. For the outdoorsy types."

I slid down to the ground. Then I grabbed a dirt clod near my feet. "Come here. I just want to see if it's even possible for dirt to cling to you."

"Do not throw that dirt clod at me."

"It's an experiment. I have to know whether you're really human! You're like the Undead. Only you're the Un-dirty!"

I did a gentle, underhand lob of the dirt clod. Rachel calmly snatched it out of the air and let it drop.

"Okay, show me your hand," I demanded. "That was wet dirt. It should have stuck to your palm."

Rachel laughed and refused to show me her hand. "So here we are. It's a beautiful Saturday morning. We have no mission, at least as far as I've heard. You going to work the rest of the day? Or are you going to come with me to the mall, buy a new bathing suit, and then come with me to the beach? I need to refresh my tan."

"My tan is already pretty fresh," I said. "And I do not want to spend the day baking in the sun while you look at guys. I have stuff to do."

Rachel crinkled her face. "Hey. What's that?"

"What's what?" I followed the direction of her stare. She was looking at an old, hand-operated water pump. It wasn't something we used. It was more of an antique that my mom liked the look of.

Attached to it was a small, silvery object. "It's a toy," I said. "A toy spaceship. *Star Wars* or *Star*

Trek or *Star Something,* I guess." I pried the little thing off the pump. "Huh. Must be magnetized."

"You look worried."

I shrugged. "Coincidence." I looked around to make sure no one was listening. "The pump is where I hid the blue box. You just unscrew the mechanism from the base plate, and it's in there."

"That's where you hid the blue box?"

"You have a better place?"

The blue box has some official Andalite name. Several, actually. It's the device they use to transfer the morphing power to an individual. A kid named David found it not so long ago. We'd used it to make him an Animorph, but David hadn't handled the power well.

David was a rat. Literally. He would live a rat, die a rat.

It wasn't something I liked thinking about. In any case, once we'd gotten the box back, I'd been the one chosen to hide it.

And now a toy spaceship was attached to it. I lifted up the silver toy and examined it. It was about three or four inches long. It was shaped like a baton, with three clusters of three long tubes at the far end and a fierce, alien death's-head bridge at the front.

I grinned at Rachel. "Romulan?"

9

"Marco would know. Or Jake. I guarantee you, either of them would be able to take one look at this toy and give you a ten-minute explanation on what show it's from and what stories it was in."

"I'll throw it in with the other Goodwill stuff," I said. I did. Then I looked up at the sky. Bright sun peeking through fluffy clouds. "Okay, I'm not a beach person, but this day is too good to waste. I'll go with you. I'll just go find a pair of my mom's Bermuda shorts to wear. The big, striped ones."

The look on Rachel's face was perfect: horror struggling with disbelief.

"Kidding," I said. "Just kidding. I'll go get my suit. You are so easy, sometimes."

CHAPTER 3

Most Powerful Emperor, Lord of the Galaxy, disaster has struck your bold minions! Our engines have malfunctioned. We searched the planet for a power source we could tap. But now, even as we replenished our strength from a strange source of transforming power, one of the alien monsters of this planet has attacked! We have sustained damage, but we are undaunted! Perhaps the weak and unworthy captain of the *Planet Crusher* will assist us so that we may achieve everlasting glory!

— From the log of the Helmacron ship, *Galaxy Blaster*

We spent a couple of hours at the beach. I have never been so bored in my life. I'm sorry, but I basically hate the beach. Still, Rachel enjoyed it, and she is my best friend.

We wore our suits home and it wasn't till I was walking up the driveway that I realized Jake was waiting.

Jake is the leader of the Animorphs. Mostly because he's the only one with enough sense of responsibility to take on the job.

And to be honest, I kind of like Jake. As in *like*. He's Rachel's cousin, and the two of them are very similar in the way both are brave and bold and decisive. But Rachel has an edge of recklessness that Jake doesn't. And Jake is almost as oblivious as I am to clothes and makeup and all that.

Jake saw us coming and looked like he wanted to hide. It suddenly occurred to me that he'd never seen me in a bathing suit. Now I wanted to hide.

"Hi!" he said, giving a little wave and keeping his eyes rock-steady on my face.

"Oh, man, this has got to be trouble," Rachel said, loudly enough for Jake to hear. "Okay, Jake, whose butt do we have to go and kick?"

Normally he would have smiled. But he just swallowed, darted a look at the rest of me, blushed, and once again, grimly focused on my face.

"He thinks I look dumpy," I muttered to Rachel under my breath.

"Cassie, you are so hopeless. What you know about guys could fit on the head of a pin. Good grief. That is not a 'she looks dumpy' look. That's a 'whoa, she looks hot, but I better not show any reaction or she'll get offended' look."

We came up to where Jake was standing. "I, uh, I brought some stuff over for you to take to Goodwill. Remember, you said I should. So I did. Some stuff and all. I gave it to your dad, and he took it. He just left."

I had to admit, this was more stammery than Jake usually got. Rachel had drifted around behind him so she could roll her eyes and do a mean parody of him looking embarrassed.

I was fighting the urge to laugh when I spotted something that made me freeze.

There was another toy spaceship attached to the water pump.

I leaped toward it. "Jake, did you get this off the truck?" I asked.

"What? No. What is that?"

I looked hard, blinked, and looked again. The toy spacecraft was back. Only it wasn't the same. This one was shorter, broader, with two big "engines" at the back instead of the clusters of smaller ones. And the death's-head bridge was different, too. Still a death's-head, but different.

"It's not the same," I said to Rachel. "It's similar, but it's not the same."

Rachel stopped rolling her eyes. Jake looked at each of us, puzzled.

And then, to our utter amazement, the little "toy" ship separated from the water pump, turned to a level position, and flew swiftly away, missing Rachel's head by inches.

"What was *that*?" Jake demanded.

Rachel shrugged. "We thought Romulan," she said.

"Jake, you know what's hidden in that water pump?"

"Of course I do." He shook his head slowly. Then he snapped into his "leader" mode. "Okay, the weekend just got canceled. Cassie, you and Rachel morph right now, get to the woods, and bring back Tobias and Ax. I'll find Marco. Back here in half an hour. Go."

CHAPTER 4

We assembled. Jake, Rachel, Marco, Ax in his own, natural Andalite body (which is a cross between a blue deer, a centaur, and a scorpion), and Tobias who, though he regained his morphing power, is a red-tailed hawk.

We assembled and tried to figure out what, if anything, we should do about a flying toy spaceship.

But, really, there were only two possible things to do. One was to talk to Ax.

"Ax, is there any way the Yeerks would use some kind of tiny, miniaturized . . . um . . . flying thing to locate the blue box?" Jake asked.

<A flying thing, Prince Jake? What is a flying thing?>

"That would be a thing that flies," Marco added helpfully.

"Like a . . . like a toy spaceship," Jake said, ignoring Marco.

<Why would they use a toy spaceship?> Ax wondered. <They have real spacecraft.> Ax kept his main eyes attentively focused on Jake, while his stalk eyes looked at Marco and me.

Jake shrugged and looked at me. I shrugged back.

Which brought us to the one *other* thing we could think of doing: going to Goodwill and finding the "toy" my dad had delivered earlier.

We morphed to seagulls and flew there. All except Tobias, who has his own wings.

We demorphed and Rachel, Jake, and I went in. We glanced quickly around the shelves and realized the toy we were looking for was not there.

I went to the clerk, a college-age guy.

"Hi. My dad dropped off some toys about a couple hours ago, along with a bunch of other stuff. And, well, it turns out we gave you some stuff we shouldn't have."

"Yeah. His toy spaceship," Rachel said, pointing at Jake.

"That's right. My toy spaceship."

"If it just came in it would still be in the back.

They would have sorted it and probably stuck it with other toys."

"Okay. Can we go look for it?" I asked, smiling my most winning smile.

"What kind of spaceship was it?" the clerk asked.

"Toy," Jake answered.

The clerk rolled his eyes. "I mean, what kind? Romulan? Federation? Klingon? Dominion? Ferengi? Or maybe it was from the *Babylon 5* universe: Minbari? Shadows? Or was it from *Star Wars*? Was it a TIE fighter?"

Rachel and I both looked at Jake.

"Romulan," he said.

The clerk jerked his thumb over his shoulder. "Back there. But don't try and grab anything that isn't yours. You better come out of there with a Romulan ship."

"Of all the clerks in all the Goodwills in the world, we have to get a science fiction fan," Jake muttered.

We went through swinging doors into a loading dock area. There was furniture piled here and there. Boxes of electronic stuff. Old TVs. A lot of old clothes and a jumbled pile of toys. Dolls, action figures, games, Legos, a tricycle. It was like all the toys of the last decade were having a convention on the cold concrete floor.

"Okay, do you see it?" Jake asked me.

I stepped gingerly around the scattered toys, picking my way over hairless Barbies and headless X-Men. Then I spotted a tangle of three toys.

"There it is!"

"Next to the Klingon battle cruiser and the G.I. Joe Attack Module?"

I rolled my eyes. "You're such a *boy*. Sometimes I almost forget you're . . . you know. I mean, it's sweet."

"Awwww." That would be Rachel, of course.

Jake sighed and went to pick up the toy spaceship. He turned it over, wrinkling his brow in puzzlement.

Then, through the open loading bay . . .

A swift, silvery machine, no more than five or six inches long, swooped into the room.

"Whoa," Jake said. "Toys have gotten so cool. I never had a toy spaceship that could —"

Tseeew! Tseeew!

"Ahhh! Owww!"

"What?" I cried, jumping to Jake's side.

He was cradling his right arm. I looked at it and saw two tiny holes burned through the sleeve of his morphing outfit.

"That little toy spaceship just shot me!"

CHAPTER 5

Most Omnipotent Leader! We have located the fools of the *Galaxy Blaster*. They have allowed themselves to be taken by the large aliens of this planet. But your loyal ship, *Planet Crusher,* will destroy all who stand in our way and will save that other unworthy ship so that they might, perhaps by mere accident, serve your great will!

— From the log of the Helmacron ship, *Planet Crusher*

The small silver ship blew past us and I saw the engine nacelles glow an electric blue. It soared up toward the warehouse style roof then turned back toward us.

Tseeew! Tseeew!

I felt two pinpricks on my left cheek. "Oww! That hurts!"

"Let's back off!" Jake said.

"Back off?" Rachel yelled. "Back off from a toy? I don't think so." She snatched up a wooden baseball bat from the pile of toys and rested it expertly on her shoulder. "Come on, you little punk!"

Tseeew! Tseeew!

"Ahhh! My hair! They shot my hair."

We all looked down in horror. There, on the concrete, lay the evidence: half a dozen long, blond hairs. The ends were still smoking.

"Okay, that's it, they're dead," Rachel said and swung the bat.

The tiny spacecraft ducked as the bat blew past, inches above it.

"I hate to say it," Jake said, unable to stifle a grin. "But since Marco isn't here to say it . . . steeeeee-RIKE one!"

"Oh, that's very amusing, Jake," Rachel snapped. "I'll laugh right after I knock these little creeps into the bleachers!"

The ship turned once more and came at us from the side.

Tseeew! Tseeew!

This time we all ducked. Rachel swung the bat blindly over her head, but missed.

"Like I said, how about if we back off?" Jake suggested.

We duckwalked back from the toy pile and the little ship landed beside the other little silver ship.

I stood up cautiously to be able to see. A bright red beam, thin as a hair, connected the two little craft.

Jake and Rachel stood up, too.

"Well, this isn't too weird," Rachel said.

"Look, the other ship is lifting off now," Jake said. "They must have given them a jump start. Just don't hit them with the bat, Rachel. Maybe they'll leave on their own."

But that was not to be. The two ships rose from the floor and hovered there around eye-level, pointing straight at us.

"Okay, have the bat ready," Jake said. "They shoot, you swing."

Then, to our surprise, we heard a thought-speak voice in our heads.

<Aliens! Give us the power source! Give it to us and we will let you live as our slaves. We will not crush and annihilate you as we will crush and annihilate all the people of this planet!>

"Power source?" Jake echoed.

"The blue box," I said, understanding it all suddenly. "That's why they were on the water pump. They think the blue box is a power source."

21

"Maybe it is, for them," Rachel said. "Not exactly polite, are they?"

We heard a second, blustering thought-speak voice. <No, we shall not let all three of you live! Only the one who brings us the power source. All others must feel the wrath of brave Helmacron warriors, the true and natural rulers of the galaxy!>

Rachel cocked an eyebrow at Jake. "Now can I hit 'em?"

I stepped forward, hoping to make peace. I held up my hands to show they were empty. I smiled. I said, "Hi, welcome to Earth. Look, some of what you're saying sounds almost threatening. And I'm sure you don't mean it that way. But —"

<Do you insult the flower of Helmacron space forces? You may insult the crew of the *Planet Crusher*, but he who insults the *Galaxy Blaster* will be smashed into little bits, and those bits ground into dust, and that dust will be blown away by the wind!>

"Ooookay. Let's try again."

Tseeew! Tseeew!

The little beams burned neat pinholes through my morphing outfit.

Then, without another word, the two tiny spaceships turned and shot out through the open door.

For about ten seconds the three of us just stared at one another. There are a lot of words for what we were feeling: Disbelief. Incredulity. Amazement.

And resentment.

Rachel said it first. "Oh, come on. Like we don't have enough problem aliens?"

Then it clicked. "The box! They're going back after the blue box!"

CHAPTER 6

"Tobias! Follow them," Jake said as we leaped from the loading dock platform onto the ground outside. "We'll be along as soon as we can."

It was time for speed. We needed to get back to the farm before the Helmacrons could manage to get hold of the blue box. We found one of the Goodwill trucks open and empty. We climbed in the back and pulled the door down to within a foot of being closed. Enough room for us to get back out when we were done morphing.

I focused on the osprey whose DNA is a part of me. I began to feel the familiar, creepy morphing sensation of pain-at-a-distance. Morphing does shocking things to your body: dissolves organs and twists bones and causes body parts to grow where no body part had been. It should be the most hideously painful experience any human has ever endured. But the morphing technology masks that pain. Like Novocain masks the pain of having your teeth drilled.

But just like when you go to the dentist, you sort of know the pain is there. I mean, you realize pain is being created, it's just not reaching your brain.

Very weird. Even in a morph you've done before, as I've done the osprey morph.

Far, far away there was the awful pain of skin blistering and forming feather patterns that grew and grew, thousands of quills erupting from my flesh. My back, my chest, my arms and legs, my face — all sprouted feathers as fast as one of those stop-action films of plants growing.

My lips grew hard as fingernails, then pouted outward to form the sharp, hooked beak. My fingers stretched and my arms shrank, and with a snap! here and a snap! there my human arm and shoulder bones became the wing and shoulder bones of a bird.

I was shrinking all the while, of course, as the dark truck grew vast around me. Two of my toes melted into the others and then turned crusty and hard. My heel bone suddenly popped through the flesh to make the rear talon.

And yet throughout all this, throughout watching my friends undergo very similar changes, we kept up a normal flow of conversation.

It's amazing what you can get used to, I guess.

<Wait a minute,> Marco was saying. <You're telling me those are actual spaceships? Three inches long?>

<Maybe four,> I said. <I didn't have a ruler.>

<Ax, what do you know about a race called the Helmacrons?> Jake asked.

<Nothing. I have heard of no such race.>

<How can aliens be that small?> Marco demanded. <It makes no sense. They'd have to have faster-than-light travel. In a three-inch-long toy spaceship?>

<They seem to disagree,> I said. <I guess they don't mind being small. They certainly seem to have a high opinion of themselves.>

<How do you mean?> Ax asked.

<Well, they say they're going to make us all their slaves,> I said. <You know, conquer the world.>

<Kind of ambitious for a bunch of sub-midgets,> Marco said.

<We do not know how large these Helmacrons are,> Ax cautioned. <They may well be any size. Perhaps these spacecraft are simply robots. Miniaturized, robotic scout vessels. The Hel-

macrons themselves may not be inside the ships. They may be elsewhere.>

<Let's quit guessing and go find out,> Rachel said impatiently. She had morphed to a huge bald eagle. She walked on her talons over to the partially open door of the truck. She ducked down, spread her wings to lower her profile, and slipped out through the gap.

I followed her, hopped down onto the bumper of the truck, and from there flapped my wings and tried to get off the ground. But it was dead air there behind the Goodwill building, so I ended up scooting along the ground for a few feet before I could get enough lift to fly.

I flapped hard to get the first few dozen feet of altitude. But once above the roofline I found a gentle wisp of breeze, turned into it, and caught some easier altitude.

The five of us flapped and circled and flapped some more till we were at a safe height, above the power lines and roofs and gas station signs.

We set off toward my farm, hoping that was the right way to go. I searched the sky ahead of me for a glimpse of Tobias. Ospreys, like all birds of prey, have incredible eyes.

But it was Rachel who spotted him, a tiny dot already halfway to the farm.

<There he is,> Rachel said. <Too far for thought-speak.>

<Let's just try and catch him,> Jake said. <Forget about staying together, everyone go for it.>

<We're too obvious bunched up like this anyway,> Marco agreed. <We look like an Audubon Society bird-recognition poster.>

To my surprise, we began to narrow the distance between us and Tobias. Which shouldn't really have been possible, since we weren't any faster — aside from Jake, in his peregrine falcon morph.

<He's stopped moving forward,> Jake reported. <He's . . . Oh, man! He's in a dogfight with one of those ships!>

Ax said what I'd only begun to think. <A Dracon beam too narrow to do more than sting a human being might have a very different effect on a creature as small as Tobias.>

Suddenly, the Helmacrons weren't all that funny.

CHAPTER 7

With osprey eyes I could see the weird aerial battle long before we reached it. Tobias was twisting and turning, flaring, diving, catching updrafts, and just generally putting on a display of flying skills.

But the two Helmacron ships were matching him almost move for move.

<Snoopy and the Red Baron,> Marco said.

It did look like some bizarre parody of a World War I fighter-pilot movie. Only instead of machine guns, the Helmacrons were firing their tiny Dracon beams. I could see singed and burned feathers. But Rachel noticed what I had missed.

<They're aiming for his eyes! They're trying to blind him!>

Jake was the first to join the battle. Rachel was seconds behind him. The rest of us caught up half a minute later.

Rachel went straight for the first ship. She hit it, talons out, raked it, spun it through the air, and peeled off to come back around.

Jake tried the same trick on the second ship but it dodged and he missed. Fortunately, it dodged right toward me. And I was mad now. They'd been trying to blind Tobias.

The little spaceship came straight for me, firing its little beams. I spilled air clumsily but managed to drop a couple of feet, whipped my wings open, caught a decent breeze, and shot up from beneath the ship.

I couldn't get my talons up so I just slammed into it beak-first.

That was not a good idea. The impact stunned me and made my vision swim.

I didn't think I wanted to try that again. But fortunately, the Helmacrons broke off and hauled butt toward Cassie's farm, just a quarter of a mile away.

We were fast birds, but the Helmacron ships were a lot faster. Now that they'd decided to avoid more bird fighting, they reached the water pump before we could really even line up to chase them.

<We have to stop them!> Rachel yelled.

But it was wings versus engines, and wings aren't going to win that kind of a race.

<Tobias, are you okay?> I asked him as we flew.

<Yeah, just a few holes here and there. They almost got my right eye but they missed. You guys got there just in time.>

Ax was in northern harrier morph not far away. <The question is: Why did they attack Tobias?>

<He was following them,> Jake suggested.

<They should have thought he was just a bird,> Ax pointed out. <Surely they can tell the difference between humans and other Earth species.>

<Are you suggesting they somehow knew what Tobias really is?> I asked.

<I do not know,> Ax said guardedly. <I am just expressing concern.>

Maybe so. But now I had concern, too. Why *had* the Helmacrons tried to shoot a bird?

No time for that now. We had to get to the blue box. But with my enhanced vision, I could already see that we were too late. The two little ships were hovering beside the pump. I could just make out the tiny little energy beams. Beams that were cutting — slowly — through the steel pump.

31

I was wearing myself out, flapping as hard as I could. But the Helmacrons just kept slicing through the metal toward the prize.

We were all about two hundred feet away when the pump simply fell over onto the ground. And sitting there out in the open, revealed for all to see, was the blue box.

We closed the distance, Jake in the lead, Rachel right behind him, the rest of us bunched up. From the two Helmacron ships came a pale, greenish beam different from the weapons. It came from the bottom of each ship as they hovered directly above the box.

The blue box moved.

<Tractor beams!> Ax yelled. <They are attempting to take the box!>

The ships rose slowly, and the box rose slowly with them. They turned, and the box turned, too.

And then Jake struck.

And then Rachel.

One ship broke off. The tractor beam failed. The box fell to the ground.

The earlier dogfight had just been a warm-up. Now things were getting serious.

CHAPTER 8

<Rachel, look out! He's on your tail!>

<I got him!>

<Cassie, turn left, left, left!>

I banked hard and twin Dracon beams missed me by millimeters.

It was sheer madness. The two silvery toy spaceships, twisting and turning and firing wildly in a melee with six birds of prey.

And all of it taking place within about a twenty-by-twenty-by-twenty-foot space in my yard. It's a good thing my parents were out.

<Cassie! Above you!> Tobias yelled.

I turned sharply, flapped, and found the ship coming down almost in front of me. I raked my talons forward, but I didn't have the speed. And worse yet, I was getting tired.

Birds of prey aren't geese. They aren't made for long flights without some relaxing soaring and gliding. And they certainly aren't made for playing air tag for twenty minutes.

We were all wearing out. It is unbelievably exhausting keeping your wings going constantly, let alone when you're in a turn ninety percent of the time.

But the Helmacrons were not tiring. And while their little beams couldn't kill us, our talons and beaks couldn't kill them, either. We could knock them around, but we couldn't penetrate their outer skin.

Rachel was the first to land. She practically fell in the dirt. She had the largest morph, the one least able to endure the turning and switchbacks.

<Can't . . .> she gasped. <Can't go on . . .>

<Aaaahhh!> Ax yelled. A Helmacron shot had hit its mark. I saw a tiny, smoking hole in his right eye. He landed, too. Demorphing would fix the wound, but I knew it must be very painful.

One of the Helmacron ships broke off the battle and went back to the blue box. But that couldn't happen.

I landed and began to demorph as fast as I

could. There are times when human is the best of all. I sprouted up from the ground and tried to catch the Helmacron with fingers only partly emerged from my wings and feet that were basically just size-six talons.

The pale green beam locked onto the blue box. The ship lifted off again, carrying the box despite the fact that the box was bigger than the ship itself.

The ship was heading toward the open barn door. Deliberately? No, that would be stupid. The Helmacrons simply didn't know they were heading into what would be a trap.

I was more and more human and now I could walk fairly well. I chased the retreating blue box.

Into the barn. Sunlight shone through dozens of small knotholes or gaps in the boards. But it was still dim and gloomy inside. The rows of smaller cages were stacked to my right. The larger cages were on my left in a single row. A rough half-wall kept the larger predators separate. Beyond them, isolated at the far end of the barn, were the horse stalls.

The horses were all out in the field. But in the barn we had half a dozen bats, two rabbits, two raccoons, a vole, a gopher, two deer, a badger, a goose, two mourning doves, a fox, three mallard ducks, a merlin, a robin, and a bluejay.

Not to mention the various rats and mice who lived there.

The Helmacron ship had come to a stop, hovering in midair. It sat atop the blue box like a hen trying to hatch an egg.

"Give up the box," I said to the Helmacron ship. "If you don't, I'll have to hurt you."

<Surrender or be annihilated!> the Helmacrons replied.

"I don't think so. In fact, I really don't think you folks are going to have much luck conquering Earth."

<We will crush you! All humans will serve us!>

"Excuse me, I don't mean to be insensitive or . . ." I searched for the right word. "I don't want to be size-ist, but has it occurred to you that we're kind of big for you to conquer? I mean, your whole ship is smaller than my foot. And your weapons don't really hurt us."

I guess this was news to the Helmacrons, because they fell silent. I thought, *Good, maybe I got through to them.*

FLASH!

I blinked and held up my hand, too late to block the flashbulb brilliance. It had been a green light of shocking intensity. I wasn't hurt, but I was definitely seeing spots.

And then I noticed something very odd.

The cages were growing larger. The animals in them were growing larger. The Helmacron ship and the blue box were growing larger.

"Oh, no," I said, more amazed than frightened. "I'm shrinking."

CHAPTER 9

I was getting small. I was getting small very fast.

I've shrunk before, when I've morphed various insects, for example. But this was new. I was shrinking as a human.

The only good thing was that at least my morphing suit was shrinking, too. Bad to be shrinking. Worse to be shrinking right out of your clothes.

"Hey!" I yelled. "What did you do to me?"

<Hah! You glory in your swollen, bloated bulk, human! You dare to defy us! We shall see how bold you are when you are the same size as we. Now you will taste bitter defeat! Now you will feel the sting of eternal humiliation!>

"I don't glory in my . . . Hey, who are you calling bloated? Wait a minute! Stop this!"

I was still shrinking. I'd started at four foot something. Now I was less than a foot tall. And I was still shrinking. I glanced over and saw a raccoon. He was bigger than I was. Not to mention a million times more hostile.

<Cassie!>

I spun around and spotted Tobias, swooping in like a 747 coming in for a landing.

"Tobias! Look out! They have a shrinking ray!"

<A what?>

FLASH!

"Never mind. You'll find out soon enough."

<Hah HAH! You all think to resist the might of the Helmacrons because you are large and because you glow with the transformational power! But we, too, know how to use the transformational power! Shrink! Shrink! And become our abject and pitiable slaves!>

<Hey,> Tobias said, sounding puzzled. <I'm shrinking. And you've already shrunk!>

"Tobias! You have to warn the others not to come in here! Somehow they're using the power of the blue box to do this."

<I can't leave you. You're less than six inches tall!>

"Warn the others!" I cried.

Tobias turned, but he was shrinking fast. He was already down to about hummingbird size. Suddenly the door was much further away for him.

<Well, this is unfortunate,> he said.

A huge, galumphing form appeared in the doorway: Marco.

"Get back!" I screamed.

But of course what he heard was, "Get back!"

FLASH!

"Hey!" Marco yelled. "No flash photography."

<Marco! Quick, before you shrink. Warn the others to stay out!>

"Say what? Before I *what*?"

But he turned and yelled over his shoulder. "Jake! Ax! Rachel! Stay out of here!"

I could see him peering down at me. His face was about the size of the Goodyear blimp — if it was about to land on top of you.

"Oh, this isn't good," he said.

I was shrinking still further. I was already as small as a cockroach. The roof of the barn already looked like it was the sky. A dim overhead light might as well have been the moon.

Marco was standing on sequoia legs, with feet the size of twin *Titanic*s.

"What's happening in there?" Jake yelled.

"Well," Marco said calmly. "The Helmacrons

have the blue box and they seem to be using it in a kind of bizarre way."

"I'm coming in," Jake said decisively.

"No!" Marco yelled in a voice that already sounded like someone breathing helium. "No, Jake and Ax, do not come in!" Then, as an afterthought, he said, "Rachel, *you* could come in."

<Marco!> Tobias chided.

"Hey, the Wicked Witch gets to be full size and I'm down here singing, 'We represent the Lollipop Guild?' I don't think so."

<Rachel, Jake, everyone stay out!> Tobias cried in thought-speak that we all heard clearly.

"Okay, everyone just stay put," Jake ordered. "Look, the other Helmacron ship took off. Rachel hit it with a brick."

I would have laughed. Only I was now shrinking down to the point where scattered bits of hay on the ground were looking like huge, felled trees. Grains of dirt were the size of soccer balls.

"I think I'm done shrinking!" I said. Not that anyone heard me. Something flew into view. Something that seemed weirdly large. Tobias. He was roughly the size of a very small fly. But he was about as big as me.

<I think I've stopped shrinking,> he said.

"Me, too."

<But we're the same size. I should be smaller than you. I started out much smaller than you.>

"I guess that's not how it works," I said. "I think the idea here is to shrink us all to the same size as the Helmacrons themselves."

Marco, now no more than three inches tall himself, came walking over. He was huge to us. But his face was getting closer all the time.

"Oh, man, you guys are small," he said. "Honey, I shrunk the Animorphs!"

"Rachel! Get a brick!" Jake said in a huge voice that reverberated around us.

CHAPTER 10

"I am loaded up and ready," Rachel said grimly.

"Give them a warning shot," he said. "Careful not to hit Cassie or the others."

Rachel must have thrown the brick, because there came a humongous earthquake.

WHAMBBBB!

It only lasted a second, but it knocked me on my butt. Fortunately, that involved a fall of only a few millimeters.

"Helmacrons, listen to me!" Jake said. "That was a warning shot. The next one lands right on top of you. Leave the blue box. Restore our people to normal size and we'll let you leave peacefully!"

43

<Never! Your brick weapon does not frighten us!>

"Yeah? Well, it banged up your other ship pretty well," Rachel said.

<Helmacrons, listen to me.> I recognized Ax's thought-speak voice. Which meant he was probably in his normal body.

Great. All I needed was for my parents to come home, find Jake and Rachel and a big blue scorpion-tailed four-eyed Deer-boy in a standoff with a toy-sized spaceship, and me the size of a gnat.

<Helmacrons,> Ax said patiently, <if you are capable of spaceflight you must also understand the fundamental laws of motion. Her weapon has a mass as great as the mass of your ship. It will be thrown at a velocity that will —>

<Do not lecture us on physics, you inferior human!>

<I am not an inferior human, I am an Andalite.>

"Hey!" Rachel said.

<Sorry,> Ax said. <I didn't mean to say that humans are inferior.>

<We will crush you, Andalite! All Andalites will grovel before us.>

<Not if my friend Rachel hits you with the dense oblong cube she is holding.>

"It's a brick, Ax. It's called a brick. We build houses out of them."

<Perhaps you should not mention that fact,> Ax said in an aside. <The Helmacrons are already contemptuous of humans.>

"Okay, I've had enough of this battle of the alien egos here. I'm counting to three. Then I'm throwing this brick. You little insects either fix my friends . . . and Marco, too . . . or you get bricked."

<Do you dare to threaten us?!>

"One . . ."

<Grovel before the might of the Helmacrons!>

"Two . . ."

Tseeew! Tseeew!

"Aaahhh!" Rachel cried.

"The other ship! It's back!" Jake yelled. "Look out!"

I could see it all happening, far, far overhead. A gigantic Rachel, holding a brick the size of a high school. The second Helmacron ship, which no longer looked nearly as tiny, came zipping in and shot Rachel in the shoulder.

She let the brick fly. But it wasn't an aimed shot. It was reflex.

The brick arced through the air, and began to drop. Straight toward us.

"Run!" Marco yelled. He was now as small as Tobias and me.

We ran. Tobias flew.

"Noooo!" Jake screamed and launched himself through the air, hands outstretched to catch the falling brick.

But then . . .

FWAPPPP!

Ax's tail blade snapped like a bullwhip, there was a shower of sparks that might as well have been the Fourth of July to us on the ground, and suddenly there were two smaller bricks tumbling apart.

I shot a look upward at the two tumbling half-bricks.

"Freeze!" I yelled.

WHAAAM!

WHAAAM!

They dropped on either side of us, once again knocking me off my feet.

Then a much heavier impact.

WHA-BOOOOM!

Jake hit the ground, fortunately missing us as well.

His face lay sideways. It was about as high as a thirty-story building. His eyes were like brown-and-white swimming pools, huge globes that looked as if they might pop and drain down like runny Jell-O.

His mouth was a valley. His nostrils were caves. When he breathed out it nearly knocked Tobias out of the air. And when he sucked in a pained inhalation it was like being near a vacuum cleaner.

I stared up, transfixed by this face I had always found attractive. And I found myself staring at a zit bigger than I was.

Fortunately, Tobias was paying attention to more important things. <Jake! Above you!>

Jake rolled over, a moving mountain, just as the two Helmacron ships, holding the blue box with twin tractor beams, attempted to fly over him.

He rolled onto his back and shot an arm about a thousand feet into the air. Fingers the size of Taxxons closed around the blue box and yanked it down.

The two Helmacron ships jerked, shuddered, but flew on.

We had the box back!

Unfortunately, Marco, Tobias, and I were still small enough to set up housekeeping inside a thimble.

47

CHAPTER 11

O Great One, Most Magnificent of all Leaders, we have met the Vast Enemy in battle and have triumphed! Using the power source we discovered, we have shrunk three of the aliens to our size. And we would have captured the power source as well, but for the cowardice of the *Galaxy Blaster*! Filled with the courage you give us, we shall recapture the power source and use it to drive our enemies before us, wailing and crying!

— From the log of the Helmacron ship, *Planet Crusher*

"Cassie? Tobias? Marco?"

Rachel's huge voice boomed. I looked up at her, so tall she could have been the Sears Tower. I wasn't sure exactly how big I was, but I had the feeling I was not large at all. For one thing, dirt wasn't dirt anymore. It was rocks.

I heard Tobias answer in thought-speak. <Rachel! Watch where you step. We're down here!>

"Down where?"

<On the ground.>

"I don't see anything."

<We're kind of small,> Tobias said.

"Kind of small?" Marco shrilled. "A termite could kick our butts."

<Very small,> Tobias amended.

"Are all three of you together?" Jake bellowed.

<Yeah. We're all together. What are we going to do?>

"I don't know," Jake admitted. "Ax?"

<I believe, Prince Jake, that the Helmacrons have a means of diverting the energy of the blue box and using it in a very different way than was intended.>

"Gee, do you think?" Marco mocked. Of course, none of them heard it because it came out, "Gee, do you think?" And even that's an exaggeration. To really convey how little sound we could make, we'd need microscopic print.

<Perhaps they should attempt to morph,> Ax suggested. <It may be that their morphs would be normal size.>

49

"Good idea," I said. "Tell them, Tobias."

<Cassie says "good idea." She's going to try it.>

I considered for a moment which morph to attempt. Something that could fly. Sitting in the dirt was not a good feeling.

"I'll go back to my osprey morph," I said. I focused my mind and began to feel the changes. The feathers . . . the talons . . . the shrinking.

The *shrinking*?

I was getting smaller. Grains of dirt weren't rocks anymore, they were mobile homes!

I reversed morph instantly. "Not a good idea," I told Tobias shakily.

<Yeah, I noticed. Um . . . Jake?>

"Houston, we have a problem," Marco intoned.

<Jake? Cassie just tried to morph to osprey but she shrank. She was on her way to being a really, really small bird. It's weird, because I'm not small. I mean, I am, but I'm the same size as Cassie and Marco. But when she tried to morph she shrank.>

<That is logical. Unfortunate, but logical,> Ax said.

"Now he's Mr. Spock," Marco said.

<The Helmacrons would have set certain size parameters, no doubt. That is to say, they picked a size and then shrank all three of them to that

size. That is now the baseline. Any morphing will be relative to that baseline.>

I thought about that for a moment, then said, "Tobias, is he saying that if we did something like morph a flea, we'd end up being microscopic?"

<Ax-man, what happens if one of us morphs a flea or something?>

<You would diminish in size. If we assume that a flea is no more than a sixteenth of an inch long normally, it would be one nine hundred and sixtieth of the height of a five-foot human. Thus, if we assume that you are currently, let us say, a quarter of an inch tall, it follows that your flea morph would be one quarter inch divided by nine hundred and sixty. Thus, your flea morph would be point-zero-zero-zero-two-six-zero-four of an inch.>

"If he says 'thus' again, I'm gonna bite him on the hoof," Marco said.

<Ax? I don't think we're a quarter inch. I think we're smaller than that.>

<Ah. Then you should make appropriate adjustments to the equation. For example, if you are a sixteenth of an inch — and that would be my best estimate — that translates as point-zero-six-two-five inches, divided by nine hundred and sixty, which would make your flea morph point-zero-zero-zero-zero-six-five-one inches.>

"How big is point-zero-zero-zero-zero-six?" I asked Marco.

"Bigger than a virus, smaller than a period," he muttered.

<No way,> Tobias said.

Then Ax said, <I would not advise morphing to flea. You would be operating at a microbial level.>

<Okay, so we don't become fleas. I didn't want to morph a flea anyway. That's not the problem. What are we supposed to do?>

"First thing is to get you guys somewhere safe," Jake said. "Then —"

"Ah! Ax, morph to human!" I heard Rachel yell. "Cassie's dad is coming!"

CHAPTER 12

"Run! It's my dad!" I yelled, and started running, stumbling across the endless plain of rocks and boulders.

"Hey! Why are you running? It's not like he'll notice us."

"Who's gonna stop him from stepping on us?"

"Aaaahhh! Run!"

We ran. Or at least Marco and I did. Tobias flew. And there came all around us a huge, stomping sound.

WHUMPF! WHUMPF! WHUMPF!

My father's footsteps.

"Jake?" my father said. "Rachel? What are you two doing here? Is Cassie around?"

"Um . . . no," Jake said. "At least . . . no."

"We came here looking for her," Rachel said. "Not here."

"Were you supposed to meet her?"

"Hello!" a new voice said quite suddenly. Ax! He must have managed to morph to human. I cringed. Ax as an Andalite was brilliant. But Andalites have no mouths. No ability to make spoken speech and no ability to taste. So Ax as a human — with a mouth — could be slightly odd.

"Hello," my dad said guardedly. "Do I know you?"

"I do not know whether you know me," Ax said. "Only you would be able to answer that question."

Then he added, "Chun. Quess-chun."

"I . . . I don't think I do know you," my father said slowly. "Why were you hiding behind that cage?"

"I did not wish you to see me," Ax said. "But now you may see me."

There was a long pause. "Ooookay," my father said at last.

"I am a friend of Cassie's," Ax offered.

"From school?"

"From school? Skuh-ool? Sss-cooool. Yes. From school. School-luh."

Meanwhile, I was running and stumbling and banging my knees on particles of dirt. Marco was right beside me and Tobias was flying along above us.

We were running flat-out. We were probably going like two feet an hour. Then . . .

WHUMPF!

"Ahhh!" Jake yelled. "Um, look out where you're going!"

"Why?" my father asked.

"Because I . . . because I . . ."

"He thought he saw a nail," Rachel said. "I thought I saw a nail, too. Ax, didn't you see a nail?"

"What is a nail? Nay-yul? Is it similar to mail?"

"Is he all right?" my father asked.

"Who, Ax? Sure, he's fine," Jake said. "He's just from a different country."

I groaned. "Oh, no, now my dad'll ask —"

"Oh, very interesting. Ax? What country are you from?"

"I am from the Republic of Ivory Coast."

"Oh, man," I moaned. "Why did I ever give him that *World Almanac*?"

"You know, if you don't mind my saying so, you don't look like you'd be from the Ivory Coast," my father said. He was getting that edge he gets in his voice when someone is slowly but surely beginning to grind his last nerve.

"How about Equatorial Guinea? The Republic of Kyrgyzstan? Canada?"

"Tell you what," my father said, "let's just go with Canada."

"I am from Canada. I am Canadese."

"Well, I think old Ax is handling that pretty well," Marco said brightly. "You'd never guess he was an alien. An idiot, maybe. Alien, no."

"How about if you kids just go on home? I'll tell Cassie you came by."

"Leave?" Jake asked, sounding panicked.

"Yes, leave," my father said in his deep, this-is-your-father-talking-and-I've-taken-all-I'm-gonna-take voice.

They didn't argue. What could they say? We heard their stomping feet as they walked off.

Then, much closer, my father's humongous feet, roughly ten football fields long, WHAM-ing around. Just ahead was a gigantic horizontal tube. The bottom bar of a cage. We ran beneath its shelter and cowered there, gasping for breath after our three-inch run.

"That is one strange kid," I heard my father mutter. "Need to talk to Cassie about that one."

Then he must have scuffed his shoe. I saw the vast, rounded front of his boot, a fifteen-story-tall hump of leather, come winging toward us.

It hit the dirt. And kicked up a small amount of dust. A few tablespoons of dirt, no more.

Just enough to bury us alive!

CHAPTER 13

I was buried in rock!

I gasped, desperate for air. But then I realized I was having no trouble breathing. The space between grains of dirt was plenty large enough for me to get air.

But how was I going to dig my way out? Some of the rocks pinning me down felt as large as I was. I say "felt" because I couldn't see anything.

I pushed against one large rock that was pressed right into my stomach. I didn't expect it to move, but it did.

I wormed my legs up so I could get my feet positioned against the rock. Then I pushed with all my might.

The rock moved. In fact, it didn't just move, I felt it pushing other rocks aside. Now there was a little, open space. I could even see a minuscule triangle of light.

I pushed against other rocks and gradually the opening widened. Suddenly, a face filled the opening.

"Oh, there you are," Marco said.

He began to dig me out. I stuck my head up out of the dirt. And, like they were nothing, I saw him lifting grains of dirt that should have weighed more than he did.

I clambered out and bent down to lift one of the rocks myself. To my shock, I could do it.

"This is amazing," I said, holding a boulder the size of a beach ball over my head.

"I know," Marco agreed with a laugh. "It's because we're small. You know, like how ants can lift things bigger than they are? Or how fleas can jump a hundred times their own height? I guess we have that same thing going on."

Tobias swooped down from high in the air — probably three or four inches. <I have it, too. I can fly higher, relatively, than before. And I bet I could almost carry one of you.>

"This doesn't make sense, does it?" I asked.

Marco shrugged. "I don't know. Later we can ask Ax."

<Actually, it does make sense because the

bigger you get, your muscles and stuff have to increase geometrically. It's like birds. Little birds can beat their wings a hundred times a minute. A bigger bird can't.>

"That's speed, not strength," I pointed out. "But maybe it's true, anyway. I mean, look how tiny gymnasts have to be. Rachel's always saying she can't do as well on uneven bars because she's so tall."

"That has to do with rotation, doesn't it? Is that the same as strength? And excuse me, but why are we sitting around having a science class when we're the size of dust?" Marco asked.

"What should we do?" I asked him.

We were sitting in what was probably a quarter-inch depression, like a shallow bowl. We couldn't see much but dirt boulders and the big cage bar above us.

"Well . . . I don't know. All I know is: We're small. We are very, very small." He brightened. "But we're strong. We could play catch with some dirt boulders."

<We should probably stay put till Jake can come back to get us.>

"I'm worried my folks will wonder where I am," I said.

"Jake will take care of that. Somehow. And we haven't exactly been gone long."

I sighed. I looked at Marco and sighed some more. It was weird. He looked like regular, old Marco. Regular, old Marco, lounging around on boulders with a monstrous, sky-blocking, horizontal steel bar over his head.

WHUMPF! WHUMPF! WHUMPF!

My father was walking by. He seemed to be heading out of the barn.

"I'm hungry," Marco said.

<Me, too. And what's my prey now? What's small enough for me to eat? A flu germ?>

And that's when they appeared over the edge of the shallow depression. A dozen of them.

Their heads were all we saw at first. They were perfectly flat on top, quite wide. From that flat top their faces came down in a sort of squashed inverted pyramid to a hooked, barbed chin. Eyes sat atop the flat heads like big green marbles that looked like they could roll off at any moment. Their mouthparts looked insectlike, with gnashing sideways teeth.

As they climbed all the way into view I could see that they were dressed in silvery, one-piece suits, covering bodies that were almost human, if you overlooked the extra set of legs. The suits had turquoise collars.

"Well, you could eat *them*," Marco suggested to Tobias.

<We are the Mighty Helmacrons of the *Planet Crusher*, the deadliest ship in the glorious Helmacron fleet!> one of the group announced. <Surrender to us now and live as our degraded beasts of burden. Or resist us and be utterly annihilated!>

They were about the same size we were. Maybe a sixteenth of an inch. And my first inclination was to burst out laughing. These characters actually thought they were going to conquer the world.

But then they raised their handheld ray guns at us. And I realized something. Their Dracon beams, or whatever they were, hadn't hurt me much when I was the size of Mount Everest, but now I was a bug.

The Helmacrons began to advance on us.

"Fight or run away?" Marco muttered.

He was looking at me. I turned to Tobias. Tobias looked at Marco.

"Boy, you miss Jake when he's not around to make the life-and-death decisions," Marco said ruefully.

Fortunately, we were spared a decision. Because now a new group of Helmacrons, this time with magenta uniform collars, came racing up from behind us.

<These are the rightful prisoners of the *Galaxy Blaster*! Stand back, you cowards, and

let true Helmacron heroes gather up their just booty!>

"We're just booty?" Marco said with a nervous giggle.

The standoff was complete. Two groups of Helmacrons, each with weapons pointed at us, but glaring at each other with their green marble eyes.

Then the cavalry arrived.

CHAPTER 14

They were gigantic. They were brown Godzillas. They were . . . cockroaches.

Their antennae were hundred-foot-long bullwhips. Their legs were jointed telephone poles. They were vast, overpowering, terrifying machines made of five-inch-thick armor.

They towered over us, two humongous, clanking cockroaches. I mean, you think you know how gross cockroaches are. But you know nothing till you've seen a cockroach literally the size of a Wal-Mart. Next time you go to a Wal-Mart or K Mart or Target or a big grocery store, stand out in front and look at it and think "cockroach."

They were very, very big.

And they didn't smell very good, either.

<Hi, it's us,> Jake said.

<You just scared the pee out of us!> Tobias answered. <Can you see us down here?>

<No, our eyes aren't very good, as you know. But Ax can see you. He led us to you.>

<Ax?> Tobias asked.

"Ax?" Marco and I said, looking at each other.

Then slowly, very slowly, we turned.

Ax.

A wolf spider.

"AAAAHHHH!"

"AAAAHHHH!"

It didn't matter that we knew it was Ax. My brain wasn't working. My legs turned to jelly. I sat down very hard, very fast.

You cannot begin to conceive of how terrifying that sight was.

Twice as tall as the roaches. With eight legs, each the size of the Saint Louis arch. Gnashing, wickedly sharp mouthparts that looked like the gates of hell. A swollen, stinking, bloated, hairy body.

But none of that was what made Marco and Tobias and me shake with uncontrollable fear.

It was the eyes.

Eight of them. Some were glittering, multifaceted compound eyes. Others were blank, dead, black simple eyes. The smallest ones looked bigger than we were.

And that face, that evil, staring face . . .

I could feel that image being laser-printed directly onto my brain. I would never forget it. If I lived a hundred years, I would be seeing that face.

<Hello,> Ax said. <Did I make an error when I said I was Canadese?>

"Ax, I hope you have control over that morph," I said.

I tried to look away and figure out how the Helmacrons were reacting, but there was just no looking away from those eight big eyeballs.

However, the Helmacrons *were* reacting.

<Do you think to terrify us with your pitiful morphs? We are Helmacron warriors!>

They were yelling this as they hustled away at top speed.

<Ax, make sure they keep running,> Jake said calmly.

Ax turned, a movement that made me yelp in fear. But at least those eyes were aimed somewhere else.

"Yuh-uh-uh-uh-uh-uk," Marco shuddered. "Man, I did not need to see *that*. That's worth about thirty nights of waking up screaming in a cold sweat."

Ax took off after the Helmacrons, jerky but swift, and as evil-looking a creation as I ever hope to see.

His lower half was obscured by the lumpy dirt around us when . . .

TSEEEEEW! TSEEEEEW!

<Aaaahhhhh!> Ax cried.

I forgot my fear and ran up the slope to see over the lip of the depression. There, hovering just a quarter inch above the dirt, was one of the Helmacron ships.

Ax twisted in apparent agony, his mile-high legs flailing madly in pure reflex. He turned toward us and then I saw the smoking, sizzling, burned-meat-smelling eye that had been incinerated by the Helmacron ship.

TSEEEEW! TSEEEEW!

They fired again, point-blank range, and all four of the legs on the left side of Ax's spider body were cut in two. He fell from the sky like some slow-motion asteroid. The severed legs toppled slowly over, like impossibly tall trees.

<Demorph!> Jake shouted. <Ax! Demorph!>

We had made a deadly mistake. It was all a question of size. The Helmacrons were laughable when we were big. But down here, at this scale, they were as dangerous as Yeerks.

CHAPTER 15

"Neep! Neep! Neep!"

A triumphant cry went up from the Helmacrons. A *spoken* cry, as opposed to their usual thought-speak.

POOMPF!

Ax hit the ground.

<Ax, demorph!> Jake yelled.

<I may crush Cassie, Marco, and Tobias as I do, Prince Jake,> Ax said. He sounded pretty calm, under the circumstances. As he well knew, if you die in morph, you die, period.

<Cassie, Marco, over here!> Jake yelled. <We'll carry you out of AAAAAHHHH!>

The second Helmacron ship had fired from behind. Jake's cockroach antennae were severed.

It was like someone cutting a power line. The falling antennae whipped around like cables.

Tobias was in the air. He might survive Ax's demorphing, but there was no way Marco and I would. And if Ax didn't demorph, the next blast from the Helmacrons might finish him.

"Marco! We have to surrender!" I yelled, grabbing his arm.

"What?"

"We can escape later. Ax has to demorph! Jake and Rachel, too. The Helmacrons will stop firing long enough to take us."

He looked furious. But he knew I was right. He shook off my arm and began waving at the closest Helmacrons.

"O mighty Helmacrons, make us your slaves! We fear your might!"

They hesitated, probably sensing a trap. But they could see that Ax was helpless. That Jake was injured.

Four of the little monsters came racing out to grab us. Up close, they gave an even more bizarre impression of being half-human, half-insect. We knew that in reality they were minuscule, but to us they seemed big enough. They kept their weapons leveled at us as they quick-marched us toward their ship.

The ship settled down all the way to the ground. It was very big at this scale. It may have seemed like a toy to us before, but now it was immense, bigger than a Yeerk Pool ship. There would be room for hundreds, if not thousands, of Helmacrons on board.

<Up, up, up!> one of the Helmacrons shouted, shoving me up the ramp that had lowered from the ship.

I ran as well as I could with Helmacrons shoving me, yanking me, pushing me.

The ramp began to move while we were still on it. I looked around and realized that Marco and I were rising up into a vast, open hangar area. To the left and right, what looked like smaller fighter ships were hanging from racks. Perhaps a dozen of them on each side.

<Ah-hah! You see our might and tremble!>

"I see your might. Where's your tremble?" Marco said.

The Helmacrons stared with their wobbly, marble eyes.

"Oh, no. We're prisoners of creatures with no sense of humor," Marco said.

<You are slaves now, aboard the glorious Helmacron ship *Planet Crusher*. We will take you to our captain. You will crawl!>

Two of the creepy little aliens shoved me down onto my knees. It didn't hurt at all, even though I felt like it should. But then, I was about the size of a large flea. I didn't exactly fall very far.

And it was weirdly easy to crawl. It was what I was starting to think of as the "insect effect." When you're tiny, it's easier to be strong. I was able to scoot along on my knees quite easily.

It was a good thing, because we crawled a long way. The ship felt like it was a mile long. Down brightly lit corridors and up ramps and across narrow bridges that spanned huge mechanical facilities of some sort, we crawled.

It was a noisy ship. Clanging and pounding and groaning. It was intensely bright as well. Far brighter than any human would find comfortable.

Finally, we seemed to have arrived. We entered a room with a dome ceiling and shallow bowl floor. In the center of the room stood a single Helmacron. Beams of light illuminated him like a movie star on Oscar night. He looked like any of the Helmacrons, except for the fact that he was wearing a flowing, gold cape.

And there was one other difference.

"He's dead," I said.

"He's about as dead as you can be," Marco agreed.

The Helmacron captain did not move. Did not breathe. His eyes did not look at us. He was covered with what looked a lot like bread mold and cobwebs.

What was worse, it was fairly obvious how he'd died. His arms and four legs were shackled, bolted to the deck. Three long, steel swords were sticking through his body. It all looked very cere-monial.

And it looked . . .

"Insane," Marco muttered. "These guys are nuts."

CHAPTER 16

O Greatest of the Great, Most Magnificent of the Magnificent, we have taken two of the strange, transforming aliens prisoner! They tremble before us! They abase themselves! They quiver in cowardly terror! And it should be noted that the *Galaxy Blaster* was of no help whatsoever.

— From the log of the Helmacron ship, *Planet Crusher*

<Grovel before the captain!>

Marco looked at me. "How do you grovel? I've never groveled before."

I shrugged.

<Grovel!>

"We don't know how," I told the closest Helmacron. "I mean, you know, different folks, different customs. Maybe you could show us."

73

They looked at one another. Then the one I'd spoken to said, <You may grovel in the style of your own people. Grovel as you normally grovel.>

I saw the sly gleam in Marco's eye. "You heard the man, Cassie. Let's grovel."

He scooted his legs forward, lay on his back, stuck his hands behind his head, and relaxed like he was at the beach soaking up sun.

"I grovel before the mighty Helmacron captain, most mighty of the mighty, undisputed champion of the world in the dust-weight category! We grovel like the pitiful losers we are! We grovel like a guy who hasn't got a date the day before the prom and the only girl around is the head cheerleader, that's how much we grovel. Cassie, you could join in any time, you know."

"We grovel . . . um, like grovelers."

Marco turned his head to shoot me a disdainful look. "Oh, good groveling. Put some feeling into it."

"I grovel like, uh . . . like a person who is really, really groveling," I said lamely.

Meanwhile, Marco was, of course, getting into it. After all, he had an audience.

"O mighty Helmacron dead guy, we grovel like a video game addict trapped in an arcade without a quarter, that's how much we grovel. You would not believe the depths of our grovelry! We grovel like a guy with a large order of fries and the only saltshaker is at the table of the school bully. We grovel —"

<Enough! Now you will tell us the location of the power source.>

"The blue box?" I inquired.

<Yes, the blue box of transforming power!>

"I don't know where it is. One of my friends must have taken it and hidden it."

<Friends?>

"Yes, the others like us. The others we were with."

<Turn on the external viewer!>

Suddenly, the entire dome ceiling lit up with a three-dimensional view of the inside of the barn. I saw Jake, Rachel, and Ax. All alive, all back in their own forms. They were glaring angrily at the ship we were in.

The viewscreen zoomed in to magnify a very tiny Tobias, sitting perched on Rachel's shoulder.

<Which one of them knows the location of the blue box?>

I was incredibly relieved that they were all apparently okay. I hoped Tobias was okay, too. Although he was obviously still small-size. There was no way we were going to put one of them on the spot.

<Which one!> the Helmacron screamed. <The one with four eyes? The one with wings?

The one with hideous blue eyes? Or the larger one?>

"None of them," Marco said. "The other one. The one who's not here."

I nodded solemnly. "Yes, the other one."

We had no idea what we were talking about, of course. But then the Helmacrons actually sort of supplied the answer.

<Do not attempt to deceive us! Our sensors reveal those who radiate with the transforming energy. We will find anyone who bears that energy signature!>

Marco and I stole a glance at each other.

"Transforming energy . . . you mean, you can tell who has the morphing power?" Marco asked.

<We are the Helmacrons, lords of the galaxy! Our science and technology are vastly superior. We can easily penetrate your simple disguises and see the transforming power at work.>

"They can tell people who are able to morph," I said to Marco. I had to resist the urge to giggle. But for once, Marco had not yet figured out what I had just figured out.

"O mighty masters," I said, "we were fools to imagine we could deceive you. There is only one other like us on this planet. Only one other who possesses the transforming power! It is he who has the blue box of transforming power. It is he whom you must find. It is he whom you must defeat!"

<We will crush him beneath us like the lowliest of creatures! He will grovel before us for an eternity of days!>

Marco still looked puzzled.

"There's no point trying to hide him from the Helmacrons, Marco," I said. "There is only one other morph-capable creature on Earth. And the Helmacrons are just going to have to destroy him."

Suddenly, the light went on in Marco's head. "Visser Three?"

I nodded, feeling very pleased with myself. "Visser Three."

CHAPTER 17

"We're going to lead them to Visser Three?" Marco asked me in a voiceless whisper.

"You have a better idea?"

"No." He shook his head admiringly. "It's just so . . . sneaky. I didn't know you had it in you."

Visser Three, leader of the Yeerk invasion of Earth, is the only Andalite-Controller in the galaxy. The only Yeerk ever to acquire the morphing power.

"Just one problem: Where do we find Visser Three?"

Marco considered. "Chances are he's on

board his Blade ship. Or on the Pool ship. Or down in the Yeerk pool. Or —"

"Do you think these guys could find the Blade ship?"

Marco shrugged. "Bigger question: What do these little guys do when they find Visser Three? Sting him with their tiny little Dracon beams?"

<You will lead us to this person who has the transforming power!> one of the Helmacrons yelled.

"He's on a spacecraft. In orbit," I said.

<Lies! Are we fools, or are we the very epitome of Helmacron courage and wisdom?> the Helmacron demanded. <We know that your pitiful species is not capable of real space-flight.>

"True," Marco said smoothly. "The person you're looking for isn't a human. See, you guys aren't the only aliens trying to conquer Earth. There are these guys called Yeerks."

This news caused a total sensation. There had been a half dozen Helmacrons in the room around their dead captain. Now many more came rushing in, all jabbering wildly in thought-speak. Some were hauling what seemed to be computer consoles of some sort. Others dragged in over-sized weapons.

There was a lot of yelling, but one thought-speak word I heard again and again was <Yeerk.>

"They know the Yeerks," I said.

"Oh, yeah. They know them, all right."

The yelling and gabbling and wild gesticulating went on at a furious pace for quite a while. Suddenly, without warning, there were steel blades flashing! Where the blades had come from, I couldn't say.

It was a sudden, violent onslaught. But not against us. There were four or five Helmacrons surrounded by all the others.

<Die, fools!> the mob cried. The swords flashed and the little gaggle of Helmacrons disappeared from our view, hidden by the wall of screaming, enraged Helmacrons.

Calm descended as suddenly as the violence had been. Through gaps in the crowd I could see Helmacrons lying dead, pierced by swords.

It was a shocking thing to experience. But the Helmacrons didn't seem very upset.

"Maybe we'd better get out of here," Marco muttered. "These guys really are insane."

"I don't think they mean to hurt us. Not yet."

One of the Helmacrons turned to face us. <Where is this Yeerk with the power source? Tell us, lowly one, or be crushed beneath our feet!>

"The Yeerks have a Pool ship and a Blade ship in orbit," Marco said. "The Blade ship is the place to start. But it's shielded, you know. Invisible to radar and sensors and all."

<Fool! We are the Helmacrons! Primitive Yeerk technology means nothing to us!>

"Of course," I said soothingly. "But you know what? Now that you know the Yeerks are here, you probably want to focus on them, not on us. So you could just let us go."

<We will drive the Yeerk usurpers before us! We will grind their flesh! They will wail in terror! The humans are ours to enslave! We are the mighty Helmacrons! Rulers of the galaxy!>

"Fine by us," Marco said.

The Helmacron shouted a command in shockingly loud thought-speak. <Male! Male, here!>

A hatch in the floor opened. And up through the floor poked a trembling head. It was like the other Helmacrons, but smaller. The flat head had a forward slant. The mouthparts were less horrifying. Still insect-looking, but smaller, gentler. The entire bearing of this creature was humbler.

<Male, take these aliens. Instruct them in the ways of obedience!>

The Helmacron shoved us toward the hatch.

"Male?" Marco wondered. "Did he . . . I mean, was that . . . is this . . ."

"I think so," I said. "The loud, hyper ones are females. This one is a male."

"Oh, man. Now I'm really scared. It's an entire species of Rachels."

CHAPTER 18

<I am your teacher in the ways of submission.>

We had been taken to a small room. Well, of course, everything was small — the room was probably about the size of an aspirin. But I mean it seemed small to us.

There were no chairs or other furniture. I guess the Helmacrons didn't mind standing. And neither did we, actually. I still felt weirdly strong because of my size.

"What's your name?" I asked the male Helmacron.

<Name?>

"Never mind."

Marco said, "How about if we call you 'wuss'? Listen up, Wuss —"

"That's not very nice, Marco," I interrupted.

"He doesn't have a name, and let's face it: He's a wuss. So, Wuss, tell me: What's the deal with the captain? He's dead."

<She. Yes, of course she is dead.>

"And why do you want your captain to be dead?"

<How else can you be sure she will not make a mistake?>

That seemed to stymie Marco. But the patient male who even I was now thinking of as "Wuss" went on to explain.

<Those who make errors must be eliminated. It is inevitable that a captain, who would make many decisions if she were alive, would therefore also make many errors. What is the point of a captain who must be killed for error? In this way we have a captain who may be respected and revered by all.>

Marco looked at me helplessly. "What's sad is that it makes a certain bizarre kind of sense." He turned back to Wuss. "How about your other leaders? All dead?"

<Yes, a Helmacron female may not ascend to a position of importance in our society unless it is certain that she will not cause prob-

lems. She must be a symbol that all can admire.>

"Kind of like *our* society," I muttered.

"Well, Wuss, aren't you supposed to tell us how to behave?"

<Yes. You must obey all females. You must wash your food before eating it. As males, you must be quiet and calm at all times.>

"I'm not male," I said. "I'm female."

<No, you are a slave. Thus you are male and must do whatever a female tells you to do.>

"Kind of like *our* society," Marco said, mimicking me.

"Is that it? That's all the rules?"

<Yes. If you fail to obey the rules, you may be killed. In fact, you may even be made captain! You will stay in this room until summoned,> Wuss said calmly. <I will leave you now.>

A door opened, the Helmacron male left, and the door closed behind him.

Marco and I looked at each other. "These people are nuts, and this is a nuthouse, and we need to bail. I don't want to be captain."

"No. No promotions, please. But we need to think. These guys are going after Visser Three, which means they'll leave Jake and Rachel and Ax and Tobias alone. All that's good. On the other hand, it seemed to me like they need the blue

85

box to create their shrinking ray. So maybe they need it to unshrink us," I reasoned.

"If they *can* unshrink us. Maybe it's a one-way thing. Did you ever think of that?"

"I don't want to think of that," I said. "I have a family I have to get back to. A life."

Marco nodded, obviously deep in thought. "If we were small like this permanently, we could grow old, have kids, and populate the world with a new race of tiny people."

"Marco, would you mind *helping*? Think of what we should do."

"Okay." He squared his shoulders. "Okay." He blew out a loud sigh. "What should we do? I don't know. Here's one thing I know: These guys are nuts. They hacked those guys down. They put dead guys in charge. They are nuts, pure and simple, Looney Tunes, whack jobs, freakazoids. They could go off on us for no reason at all. So priority number one is to *not* help them get Visser Three. Priority number one is *let's get outta here*."

"I have to agree. First chance we get. But right now we're probably in space on our way to find the Blade ship, so there isn't exactly anywhere to go."

The door opened quite suddenly. It was a swaggering female. <Come with me, insignificant aliens! Obey me!>

"Yes, ma'am!" Marco said.

We were led back to what had to be the ship's actual bridge. There was no captain, dead or alive. The Helmacrons seemed to do their jobs without being told. Although obviously there were occasional disagreements, as we had seen.

<Screen on!> our Helmacron guide snapped.

A video display showed a flat two-dimensional image of Visser Three's Blade ship.

"Wow," Marco said, genuinely impressed. "You guys are fast. I mean, you ladies. You found the Blade ship!"

<We are the Helmacrons! Yeerk pretenders and usurpers will beg for their lives as we march over their groveling, prostrate forms!>

I formed a mental image of a Yeerk I'd seen in its natural form. And then of an army of tiny little Helmacrons marching over it. It would look roughly like ants on a dog doo-doo. I barely stifled a giggle.

<We have found the weak and pathetic Blade ship! But a smaller Yeerk craft has detached and is heading toward the planet surface. Our sensors show a person aboard that smaller vessel, a person who carries the distinctive sensor signature of the transforming energy!>

"Visser Three," I said. "He's heading down to the planet. Probably heading down to take the blue box. I mean the power source."

The Helmacron ship was obviously in hot pursuit. We could see a Bug fighter dropping down through blue atmosphere. Our own familiar coastline was recognizable below us.

The sun was going down. The line of darkness was marching across the earth, getting nearer to my own home.

It suddenly hit me just how far away I was from the life I knew. Not just in miles, but in feet and inches, too. My parents were gigantic, skyscraper-tall behemoths. Marco and I, and maybe Tobias, were alone in the universe.

<Tell us of the place the Yeerk Bug fighter is landing!>

I peered at the screen. "Can you make it bigger? I mean, you know, magnify it?"

The screen jerked as the picture refocused closer in.

"Hey, look!" I said. "Very interesting."

I could see a stretch of the boulevard that ran by our school. It was one of those commercial strips with tons of fast-food restaurants and muffler shops and banks and Blockbusters.

An empty, abandoned restaurant — I think it used to be a Denny's or something — stood by itself, surrounded by a weed-grown parking lot.

The Bug ship, invisible to humans thanks to its shielding, was settling down toward the empty restaurant.

As we watched, the roof of the restaurant split and opened, drawing back like a pair of sliding doors.

The Bug fighter containing Visser Three slowly, carefully, landed in the interior of the building. The roof closed behind it. And at that moment a long, black limousine came tearing into the parking lot.

"Very clever," Marco said admiringly.

"It's an empty building," I told the Helmacron. "The Visser will morph to human form and leave in that black vehicle."

<Then we will crush him there! We will annihilate him! We will humble his pride till he weeps and begs for an honorable death.>

"Uh-huh," Marco said dryly. "We've tried that before."

CHAPTER 19

O Great One, Most Bold of Leaders, we grovel before you, though we are light-years away. It is our sad duty to report that the treacherous jackanapes of the *Galaxy Blaster* have run away! They have seized two alien prisoners that were rightly ours and run away! Leaving us, your loyal warriors, to battle the large aliens as we search for the blue box of transforming energy.

— From the log of the Helmacron ship, *Planet Crusher*

"It's like *Lethal Weapon 5*," Marco said. "This is cool! This is the ultimate weird chase scene."

Visser Three had morphed to human and entered the limousine. We'd seen him do this before. I guess he liked limos because behind the blacked-out glass he could morph or demorph without being seen.

And there might be other, crueler things he did in there. Visser Three was not exactly kind to his underlings.

The limo glided down the boulevard. Night was coming, and already the neon lights were lit. Reflections of golden arches and big yellow mufflers slid over the oily black curves of the limo. The word *Mobil* slithered like a blue-and-red snake.

An ambulance went wailing past. Minivans full of parents and kids kept pace with the long black car carrying the most dangerous creature on Earth. Or any other planet.

We saw all this clearly because the screens were on all around the bridge. And we were flying right along, just slightly behind and beside the limo. We were maybe four feet from the back right-side window.

Suddenly, the *Galaxy Blaster* took a hard jerk left and fired.

TSEEEEW! TSEEEEW!

What looked to us like huge, thick beams of light lanced toward the window. But of course the window was a smooth, black cliff to us. The

Helmacron viewscreens didn't magnify — they shrank. They diminished. So as the beams traveled, they seemed to shrink to bright, insignificant hairs.

<Ahhh! Die, Yeerk! Feel our might!> The Helmacrons yelled like fans at a football game whose team had just scored a home run. Or whatever it is they do in football.

<Again! Again! Punish the arrogant Yeerk usurper!>

TSEEEW! TSEEEW!

Once more there was giddy cheering and excitement. And then the window of the limo began to lower.

A puzzled, human face looked out at us.

Visser Three! We knew his human morph. It was Visser Three, unable, even in human guise, to conceal the dark evil within.

But right now he didn't look frightening so much as puzzled. I saw his huge human mouth form the word "What?" And then slowly the expression turned to amazement.

"Helmacrons?" the mouth said silently.

<What words is the creature speaking?> the nearest Helmacron demanded of us.

"He said 'Helmacrons?'"

<Ahhhh! Yah-haaaah!> the Helmacrons crowed in thought-speak. And from their nasty little insect mouths came "Neep! Neep! Neep!"

<Now feel your terror grow, Yeerk!>

TSEEEW! TSEEEW!

The *Galaxy Blaster* fired, point-blank, at a face that could have been King Kong looking in the window of a skyscraper.

Visser Three's human hand slapped his face and came away with two little spots of blood. He stared at the blood for a few seconds, and then his eyes, seething with rage, glared at us.

<See the helpless, quivering terror in him!>

"You see any helpless quivering there?" I whispered to Marco.

"No. That is one p.o.'ed Yeerk."

And that's when the chase scene turned deadly.

The limo took a sudden swerve. The wall of steel and glass and the huge malevolent face all came flying toward us, irresistible as a tidal wave.

The *Galaxy Blaster* reversed and pulled away, but it was a close call.

I saw the bizarre sight of a human the size of the Matterhorn rising from the roof of the limo.

"Sunroof!" Marco said. "It's a human-Controller coming up out of the sunroof."

In the Controller's hand, a gun. And I hate to keep obsessing over size, but the gun he leveled at us was not like a cannon. A cannon would have been a BB gun compared to this thing.

You have to understand, we were a sixteenth of an inch tall. The bullet that would have come flying from that gun was probably ten or twelve times longer than we were tall. I'm a little over four feet, so the equivalent would be a bullet like forty or fifty feet long.

A forty-foot-long *bullet.*

BOOOOM!

Flames exploded from the gun barrel. Flames like a volcanic eruption. And that bullet the size of a Greyhound bus came flying straight for the *Galaxy Blaster.*

CHAPTER 20

The *Galaxy Blaster* jerked with lightning speed. The biggest bullet in the universe blew past, leaving a brief tornado in its wake.

<He dares to attack us! Unprovoked attack! The foul beast will curse the day he was born!>

Marco looked at me. He was shaking. So was I.

TSEEEW! TSEEEW!

BOOOOM! BOOOOM!

The limo swerved madly. The little ship swerved even more madly.

We lofted up over the top of the limo. The human-Controller was directly beneath us, raising his gun.

TSEEEW!

We fired and the man slapped his head in annoyance.

BOOOM!

Another sperm-whale-sized bullet went rocketing past.

Of course, throughout all this, the Helmacrons kept up their lunatic cheering and yahhooing and neep-neeping. The extravagant threats and insults flowed constantly.

And then things got bad. The ship went over to the far side of the limo.

"No, you idiots! Oncoming traffic!" Marco screamed.

Through the screens I saw the horrifying sight of a car coming right for us. It was a sport utility kind of thing. Each of the bright, polished bars of the grill could have been an Empire State Building.

"Pull up!" I screamed.

<Up! Up! Up!> some of the Helmacrons shouted.

<Down! Down! Down!> others shouted.

The *Galaxy Blaster* shot downward. But the four-wheeler was coming at us at an incredible closing speed. A bumper the length of a coastline filled the screen.

And then, by a millimeter, we slipped beneath it. Wheels flashed by. Wind whipped at us. We blew out beneath the back bumper.

Another car was right ahead of us. But the Helmacrons had decided the disagreement over "up" and "down" required some more correction of error. The long swords flashed.

I shrank back against the curved bulkhead and hauled a horrified, fascinated Marco with me.

"We have to get out of here," I said. "Now."

"I'm with you. But how?"

"We have to morph."

"Morph? These guys see right through morphs. We morph wolves or whatever, they'll just shoot us!"

"It's all about size," I said grimly. "We can't get big enough to fight them. But we can get small."

"No, no, no, no," he said, shaking his head.

"No other way."

"We don't even know what'll happen!"

"We have to find out."

He shuddered. "What, flea?"

I shook my head. "Flea is too out of control. Besides, their senses are weak. I think fly. Very, very tiny flies."

He nodded reluctantly, clearly afraid. It's not like I could blame him. We'd morphed flies before. But we were going to be going to a dimension neither of us could even imagine.

Our baseline size was a sixteenth of an inch.

If we morphed flies, we'd be smaller in proportion.

And that was very small.

I focused my thoughts, even as another idiotic cheer broke out from the Helmacrons.

I looked at Marco. He was shrinking. So was I.

I saw the spiky hairs shoot from his back. I saw a middle set of legs sprout from his chest with a wet sound. His mouth twisted and began to push out. Out and out, into the long, sucking, sponging mouthparts of a fly.

I was still looking at him when the bulging, glittering, multifaceted fly eyes popped out of his face.

Just then, the nearest Helmacrons noticed what was happening.

<You will cry for all eternity for this!> they yelled.

They closed in around us. But now the Helmacrons were big, clumsy, slow-moving behemoths. They reached for us and missed.

And still we shrank.

CHAPTER 21

We shrank down toward the seemingly smooth deck. But just as the dirt had become rocks and boulders the first time we shrank, the smooth metal floor was now becoming a rugged plain of weird shapes, upjutting points, and cauliflower extrusions.

I was seeing it all through fly eyes. A hundred TV sets, each seeing the same scene from slightly different angles.

The colors were weird. They always are when you're in fly morph. But now I was seeing things not even flies see.

A huge Helmacron hand came reaching down from heaven to grab me. But as it neared I

99

shrank faster and faster. And by the time it came its closest, I wasn't looking at flesh anymore.

I was seeing individual cells.

<Aaaahhhh!> I yelled in shock.

<Oh, man!> Marco yelled. <Biology class!>

The wall of cells seemed to be moving in slow motion. Slower and slower. As we got smaller, we got faster. Faster and stronger, relatively speaking. Just as we had when we'd become humans a sixteenth of an inch tall.

The Helmacron hand moved through molasses. The cells of the finger were like irregular bricks in a wall. But these bricks were bigger than we were. A lot bigger.

Some were clearer, more translucent than others in the bizarre light. Some I could see right into. They were like clear plastic trash bags stuffed with faintly pink Jell-O. Suspended in the Jell-O like so much fruit cocktail were all the cell structures: a big nucleus, only slightly darker than the protoplasm, mitochondria, vacuoles . . .

<So, that's what a ribosome looks like,> Marco said. <They aren't all different colors, like in the textbooks.>

<Who knows what color anything is with these eyes and in this light?>

Slowly the wall of cells receded, leaving us as

the smallest flies anyone had ever imagined. We were flies smaller than a skin cell.

<Well, they can't catch us,> Marco said. <But now what are we supposed to do?>

<Get away?> I said doubtfully.

<If we fly for a few weeks we can probably make it two or three feet,> Marco said grimly.

He was right. Maybe. <On the other hand, this ship can smash into a brick wall and it probably won't hurt us.>

<We still have a two-hour limit on this morph. And there's no way we're staying in this morph!>

<Hey! We hitch a ride!> I suggested. <Grab that Helmacron finger.>

We fired our wings and took off. I don't know how far away the finger was in actual distance, but it seemed near enough to us. We flew at shocking speed and caught the wall of cells. My fly feet grabbed on easily enough, and then slowly the cell wall continued to rise away from the floor.

But now, with the cell membrane directly beneath my feet, I noticed something very unsettling.

<It's . . . like vibrating,> I said. <The ground. I mean, the cell wall. It's . . . vibrating.>

<Yeah. And I don't even want to tell you why.>

101

<Tell me.>

<I think those are individual molecules we're seeing. I mean, not actually seeing, but the way it looks like on a TV screen up real close? All the tiny, shifting, vibrating dots? I think those are molecules.>

I felt sick inside. Fascinated, amazed, but sick. <We're small.>

<Oh, yeah. We are seriously small.>

<And that's not the only problem we have. The cell we're standing on is about to divide.> Looking down through the buzzing surface of the cell, I could see the nucleus beginning, oh so slowly, to pinch in two.

<Look! The sky!>

From above us a new wall of cells was approaching very slowly. It was coming down toward us at an angle. But a line of darkness was moving across the landscape.

<I think we may be upside down now,> I said, trying to make some logical sense of the direction of the light. <I think . . . I think that surface above us is actually below us.>

<Let's get off this finger.>

<Why?>

<Because human or Helmacron, you just never know where a person's gonna stick their finger next,> he said.

I took about three seconds to think about

that. I shuddered. <Thanks for that image, Marco. Let's try for that surface up there. Or down there.>

I fired my fly wings, and even this tiny, the fly could live up to its name. It flew. And it flew like a rocket. A fly is always acrobatic. But now it seemed amazingly fast as well.

Maybe it was all an illusion. Who knows? Nothing made sense at this scale. But I felt like someone had tied rockets onto our hairy thoraxes and lit them up.

We blew through the air, heading up, down, sideways, whatever direction it was.

We flipped in midair and landed on the new surface. It was much like the finger. But we could hope it was safer in the long run.

As the finger slowly pulled away, we looked around our new location. It seemed to be an endless, flat plain. But towering impossibly high above us was a globe the size of a green moon. We could only guess at its extent because it stretched away in all directions. All we could tell was that the wild, rough surface, made up of extravagantly colored cells, was spherical.

<Eyeball,> Marco said. <I think we're on some Helmacron's head. And that's an eyeball.>

We were gazing up at this sight when the eye blazed a brilliant red. I could see the individual eye facets close in rapid response.

But it was more than light.

A wave of heat propelled on a hurricane came rolling across the Great Plains of the Helmacron's head.

And across the flat head of the Helmacron came something no human eye would ever see. At least not in all its horrifying detail.

I think we both knew right away what it was. But your mind doesn't want to believe what it's seeing.

The flash had been the light of a Dracon beam. Light is light, of course, and is equally fast whatever size you are.

But as the wave of energy spreads through the body hit by a Dracon beam, the physiological reaction of cells blowing apart happens more slowly.

Ax explained to us once that this was a unique Yeerk technology. The Andalite shredder whose technology the Yeerks used in developing the Dracon beam kills instantly, painlessly.

The Dracon beam is specifically modified to destroy more slowly. The Yeerks want their enemies to feel the agony of cells exploding.

And now, standing there on cells whose molecules vibrated beneath our fly feet, we saw the line of destruction advance. Cells erupted, exploding like mini-geysers, swelling with steam, blowing nuclei and mitochondria and flaming cytoplasm like shrapnel.

<MOVE!> Marco bellowed, breaking me out of my horrified trance.

I fired the fly's wings and rose off the skin just as the line of explosion rolled beneath us.

CHAPTER 22

Tornado winds, so hot they singed our wings, caught us and threw us through the air. We slammed into each other and instinctively grabbed hold, fly feet clutching fly hairs.

We were thrown like meteors, rolling and tumbling out of control through the air.

Everywhere there was fire. Everywhere there was deep, pounding bass drum noise. We were in a whirlwind that moved with weird slowness and impossible-to-resist force.

We must have been knocked unconscious. Because it felt like much later when I next heard Marco's thought-speak voice.

<Dracon beam!> Marco said. <The Yeerks must have hit the ship.>

<We were in the middle of a busy highway,> I said, still clutching tight to a fly and thinking its foul body was all the salvation in the world.

<I think the wind is dying down. Heat is lower,> Marco observed.

Still we held tight, till slowly, slowly, the wind did die down, the blast furnace heat lessened. The mad chaos subsided.

We separated at last and flew side by side through the air. Were we still in the ship? Was there a ship? There was no way to tell. Nothing was close enough to see.

We could be anywhere. We could be an inch above the ground or a hundred miles up. We could be within six inches of a person or the last creatures left alive in the universe.

<We have to demorph,> I said.

<We could be anywhere,> Marco said. <We could be in the middle of that highway with a truck bearing down on us.>

I tried to look around, using my fly eyes. But fly eyes aren't great at distances. Flies have no need to see far. I tried out the sense of smell, but it was like it had been turned off. The scent molecules I would normally have "tasted" were probably too large, relatively speaking, for me to make sense of.

<If we demorph slowly we'll settle toward the ground as we gain weight,> I said.

<Unless the truck hits us.>

<I'll go first,> I said.

<Don't go all heroic on me,> Marco said with a laugh. <If we're gonna get hit, we'll get hit together.>

I focused my thoughts, fighting down the fear. And fighting down, too, the urgent desire to get as large as I could as fast as I could.

I felt the changes begin and I backed off. I was larger, three or four times what I had been. And now I could better feel the direction of gravity. But even with my wings held immobile, refusing to answer the instinct to fly, I floated through the air.

I demorphed a bit more. I was now dozens of times larger than I had been to begin with, but not all the way back up to the sixteenth of an inch size.

I was definitely dropping now. I could feel the direction of gravity. I knew up from down. I fell, but slowly. The air still buoyed me up, as well as the most wonderful thermal.

Now, however, my human eyes began to replace the compound eyes of the fly. I saw Marco, like me, a hideous mix of fly and human, half-falling, half-drifting, on the breeze.

Then, far beneath us, I saw the ground. Or at least what might be the ground.

I felt like a parachutist in free fall, spinning and falling, spinning and falling toward the ground. Only instead of a square patchwork pattern of cornfields and roads, I saw what looked like a nest of gigantic snakes reaching up out of the distance.

<Oh, that looks good,> Marco muttered.

But now the breeze was blowing us across the huge snakes toward an area that was more open. It was like an endless pink plain, curved away toward the horizons.

I let myself demorph some more. What other choice was there?

I fell faster, but still slowly. I could see the snakes were a bit smaller, though still monstrous. And rather than being snakes, they looked like unbelievably long palm trees.

They were planted in the ground a few miles down. They had rough, slender, waving, bent trunks. And at the top they split in two or three and became rougher.

<Oh, my God, they're hairs,> I said. <We're landing on someone's head.>

<Or armpit,> Marco said.

We came down at the edge of what seemed like a forest on one side and an endless plain on the other.

We fell down through a widely spaced thicket of the rough-textured hairs, down, down toward the scalp below.

It became darker down in the hair forest. And we were not alone.

There were no bright eyes blinking at us from the dark, like in some cartoon jungle. No, the creatures we passed had no eyes. They clung to the scalp at the base of the giant hairs and almost seemed to be waiting for us as we fell.

Eight-legged, clumsy, clanking, awful beasts. They were there by the hundreds. Everywhere around the base of the hairs. In the normal world they were too small to be seen. But to us they were as big as dogs.

<Mites,> I said, fighting an urge to throw up. <Everyone has them.>

<Let's get big, right now!>

We demorphed the rest of the way, rocketing back to our sixteenth of an inch height. Just as we landed between a pair of mites.

We were now far bigger than the mites. They were like rats to us. And they were not aware of us, interested in us, or able to respond to us.

Still, those hideous mechanical things scared me down deep inside.

Fully human once more, we ran at full speed toward the line of hair and scalp.

<Thank goodness they haven't totally cured baldness yet,> Marco said as we rushed, panting, out onto open, pink scalp.

We could see again. Like humans. And we could hear.

What we heard did not make us feel any better.

<A Helmacron ship,> Visser Three said. <It's almost . . . cute . . . what's left of it. Hah hah HAH!>

Then a human voice vibrated up through the scalp, resonating beneath us like the biggest sound in the world.

"Congratulations on your defeat of them, Visser!"

<Pah! Defeating Helmacrons is no great honor, Chapman.>

I looked at Marco. He looked at me. "Chapman?" we both said at the same moment.

We were on Chapman's head. Chapman, our vice principal. Chapman, the head of The Sharing.

Partly bald Chapman.

<Oh, there you are!> a thought-speak voice said.

111

I jumped about three feet. Or maybe a thirty-second of an inch. My heart was in my throat before I registered the familiarity of that "voice."

<I've been looking all over for you guys,> Tobias said calmly as he swooped down from the sky an inch above us.

CHAPTER 23

"Tobias! What are you doing here?" I yelled in sheer joy at seeing him. I also yelled because although hawk hearing is better than human hearing, we were still very small.

<You're standing on Chapman's head and you want to know what *I'm* doing here?> He laughed. <You had us worried.>

"How did you find us?"

<The other Helmacron ship. The *Planet Crusher*. Rachel managed to smash it with a tire iron. Knocked it down. Jake grabbed it and clamped it into that vise in Cassie's barn.>

He landed beside us, sinking his talons into scalp.

"The one my dad uses to hold wood he's working with?" I asked. My father has a small tool bench in the back of the barn. He uses it to repair cages and fix the barn itself. There's a large vise mounted on the tool bench.

<Yeah, he got 'em in the vise and kept squeezing till they agreed to help us.>

"You didn't trust them, I hope," Marco said.

<We're not idiots. They gave us hostages. Their captain and a bunch of other high-ranking —>

"NOOOO!" I yelled.

"You *are* idiots!" Marco cried. "All Helmacron leaders are dead! They don't trust anyone living, so all their leaders have to be dead!"

<Say what?>

"Just go with it," I said. "Are Jake, Rachel, and Ax here, too?"

"And where is *here*, by the way?" Marco asked.

<Yeah, they're all here, but in morph. It's a meeting of The Sharing. Visser Three is here at the secret part of the meeting. You know, where only the leading Controllers attend. He's playing show-and-tell with the *Galaxy Blaster*. He smoked it with a Dracon beam, I guess. He's holding it up and babbling about the Helmacrons. Chapman is applauding.>

Now that I thought about it, I could feel a sort of concussion that translated up through Chapman's head. It might be clapping.

And if I looked hard toward the horizon, I could see the tops of other heads. Kind of like a chain of mountains in the distance.

There was a continuous rumble of noise. Speaking voices and occasional applause.

Suddenly, I had a terrible premonition. "Where's the blue box?" I demanded.

<Well . . . Ax has it. We're in that old meeting hall The Sharing uses sometimes,> Tobias said. <Ax is outside in human morph. He's waiting till we rescue you guys. Then we're going back to the Helmacrons to get them to unshrink you.>

"Why would you bring the blue box *here*?!" Marco raged.

<The Helmacrons want it bad. We couldn't be sure we could hide it well enough from their sensors. So we had to bring it with us. We can't lose it. After all, the Helmacrons need it to unshrink you guys, which they've promised to do, and —>

"Oh. NO!" I said. "The Helmacrons tracked the *Galaxy Blaster* and told you where it would be. Then you guys came here with the blue box? Don't you see? The Helmacrons are going to try and take the blue box! They figure we'll be too busy fighting Yeerks to stop them!"

<But they're back at the barn . . . and . . . oh, man! Ax! We have to get to Ax! He's in human morph with human eyes! He doesn't even realize he has to look behind him!>

Tobias flapped his wings and caught air. He began to fly away, leaving us stranded on the vast, mostly empty plain of Chapman's head. But Tobias didn't get far.

<Now we shall destroy all who oppose us!> the familiar, blustering Helmacron voice shouted. <All will cringe and cry and wail and rue the day they first drew breath!>

It flew in low, skimming just a few inches over Chapman's head. I looked up and saw it zip past. It was the *Planet Crusher*.

And it was carrying the blue box.

<Now shall we avenge our bold and brave comrades of the *Galaxy Blaster* who died like great heroes!>

I looked at Marco. "Brave and bold? They despised the *Galaxy Blaster* and vice versa."

Marco rolled his eyes. "The *Galaxy Blaster* has been destroyed. Now they're cool. I'm telling you these guys are nuts."

The *Planet Crusher*, straining to carry the blue box, stopped and hovered just a few inches over Chapman's head. Chapman's head began to turn, following the ship.

The scalp dome tilted down. Down till we

could see over the edge of our little world. And there stood a vast, dim, but unmistakable figure.

Visser Three.

Looking unhappy, as well he should. Because the *Planet Crusher* was aiming right at him.

They fired! The green flash beam bathed the Visser in its light, and as we watched, he began to get smaller.

CHAPTER 24

O Most Magnificent and Omnipotent One! We have taken the blue box of transforming power! Though the blessed and glorious heroes of the *Galaxy Blaster* are gone from us, we of the *Planet Crusher* shall avenge them!

— From the log of the Helmacron ship, *Planet Crusher*

Visser Three literally began to sink from sight.

Chapman immediately made a mad grab for the little ship, but it skipped away easily from his groping fingers.

There was a lot of loud yelling, but no one stopped the little ship from firing again. Again and again.

<Jake! Rachel! Ax!> Tobias yelled in thought-speak. <We have problems here! Like right *now*!>

But I guess they already knew about it. It was hard for me to make sense of what I saw, since I was watching the movement of shapes so vast they might as well have been planets.

But I did make out a humongous wall of gray and pale feathers go flying past, shockingly close to Chapman's face. It was a peregrine falcon that could have swallowed a blue whale, from my perspective. Talons so big it would take me five minutes to walk from end to end of them came flashing out, reaching for the Helmacron ship.

It wasn't about saving Visser Three, of course. It was about the blue box. That box could not fall into Yeerk hands. Indeed, as he shrank, becoming an ever smaller and smaller Andalite-Controller, Visser Three cried out in anguished thought-speak.

<The blue box! The morphing cube! Get it! Get it you fools! Nothing else matters, get that box!>

Total pandemonium followed as huge, shadowy creatures rushed to and fro around our perch on Chapman's head. There was Jake in his falcon morph, dodging and swerving at incredible speed (although it seemed pretty poky to us), trying to snatch the box from the Helmacrons.

There was Ax, back in his own proper, monstrously large Andalite body, his stalk eyes looking like big, green swimming pools.

And Rachel, so big it looked like her shaggy bear head must be scraping the stars out of the sky.

Human-Controllers ran here and there. I even thought I saw a flash of Hork-Bajir horn rushing past.

It was like this awesome dance of giants. A titan hoedown. And everyone was yelling.

<Rachel! Grab it!> Jake yelled.

"Get the box! Get the box!" various panicked Controllers yammered.

<Get the box or I'll make every one of you suffer!> Visser Three yelled in enraged, impotent thought-speak.

And of course, the Helmacrons would not shut up. <Scurry in heedless terror, pathetic weaklings! It will not save you from our righteous wrath!>

Everywhere hands and talons and claws were grabbing at the ship. But nothing seemed to connect. Even slowed by carrying the weight of the blue box, the Helmacrons were faster than the blundering mob of Controllers and morphed Animorphs.

<Struggle in vain, pitiful, inferior creatures! All will serve to burnish the everlasting glory of the Helmacron Empire and its mighty warriors!>

Jake, Rachel, Ax, and Tobias were thought-speaking so that only we and they could hear. What they had to say wasn't encouraging.

<Rachel! Look out behind you!>

<I got him! No, I don't!>

<Prince Jake, it is coming your way!>

<Aaaahhhh! No! No! No! They got me. I'm shrinking! The treacherous little —>

"We have to help," I told Marco, grabbing his shoulder.

"Help? What are we gonna do? We couldn't beat a mad mitochondrion!"

<Oh, man! I'm getting small!> Rachel cried. <I am so going to kick Helmacron butt!> Then, a few seconds later, <Okay, now this is *way* small.>

"They're going to get all of us!" I cried. I have seldom felt so desperate and helpless. What could we do? What could a pair of ant-sized humans do?

Then I had a brilliant idea. Or at least an idea.

"Marco, I have to morph! I have to be able to thought-speak. And you and I have to get even smaller!"

I focused as well as I could and began to morph to skunk. It was plenty small without being subcellular like a fly. As soon as I was able, I cried out frantically to Tobias.

<Tobias! You have to come and get me and Marco!>

121

<Why not? I can't do anything else,> he cried in utter frustration. <The Helmacrons are busy trying to shrink everyone they see. And the Controllers are all chasing them around, trying to grab the blue box. They're ignoring me! I'm not a threat! But you guys are too big for me to carry.>

<Not anymore.> I was shrinking rapidly, shriveling from a sixteenth of an inch to something far smaller. But at least I couldn't see the buzzing of individual molecules at this size.

That was way too creepy.

Marco followed my example, morphing rapidly to mole. Tobias came swooping down to us, himself a sixteenth of an inch long, but now quite large compared to us. He took us up, one in each big talon, and flew away.

<So do we have a plan?> he asked.

<Yeah. It's all about size, and we keep forgetting that,> I said. <We were shrunk to Helmacron size. A sixteenth of an inch or so. And when we morph something smaller, we shrink from that base height, right?>

<Either that or I've been having a really bad dream,> Marco said.

<Okay then. How about if we morph something bigger? Shouldn't we get relatively larger?>

<Hey, yeah!> Tobias said. Then, <So what?>

<So you said the Helmacrons are ignoring you, since you've already shrunk,> I said.

<Yeah. Again, so what?>

<So . . . do you think you can land on the Helmacron ship?>

CHAPTER 25

We clung to Tobias's legs, crawling up into his lower feathers so he'd have the use of his talons.

And then we flew.

It was still a melee. Human-Controllers were chasing the Helmacron ship, trying to grab the blue box. The Helmacrons responded by firing their ray and shrinking anyone who came too close.

But they didn't fire at Tobias. He was no threat. Or so they believed.

<I think I can get them!> Tobias yelled as the ship came swerving toward us.

It shot beneath us, then paused to aim and fire.

In that few seconds of hesitation, Tobias went into a stoop, folding his wings back and dropping like a stone. Or at least like a large grain of sand.

He landed on the top of the seemingly huge Helmacron ship. The surface was encrusted with tubes, equipment, sensor arrays, and various other details, so his talons found a hold.

Then the ship was off again, zipping wildly through a forest of reaching hands.

<See the pitiful efforts of the Yeerk usurpers! They imagine that they will be masters of the galaxy. Hah! It is we, the Helmacrons, who must rule all!>

And frankly, they *were* pretty pitiful efforts. No one was going to shoot as long as the Helmacrons had the blue box. Everyone was focused on it and it alone.

<Okay, now what?> Tobias asked me.

<Now we morph. You morph to human. Your human morph should be in proportion to your natural hawk size. You should be at least a quarter inch tall! That's a lot of extra weight for this ship to carry on top of carrying the blue box.>

<It may slow 'em down,> Marco said. <But will it stop them? And even if it does, the Yeerks will be able to grab the blue box.>

<I don't think it will stop them,> I admitted. <But *my* morph will. Let's see how well they fly with a humpback whale sitting on top of them!>

<Um, Cassie?> Marco said. <How is a three- or four-inch whale going to hold onto a ship?>

<I'll wedge myself between the engine nacelles. The bigger I get, the tighter I'll be wedged.>

<Let's give it a try,> Tobias said. And he began to morph to human.

Morphing is always frightening and disturbing and nightmarishly weird. But this was a new experience. I was *on* someone morphing. I sat there, clinging with my little skunk paws to Tobias's feathers as they began to melt away.

I slipped and landed on his middle talon as it swelled and grew and became smooth in texture. I was right there, inches away, when the toes began to grow. It was like being in the middle of an earthquake. The "ground" rumbled and shook.

Tobias rose, taller and taller, but as he grew he bent low, clinging with still-forming hands to the ship beneath us.

Marco and I began to demorph as well. We would have been a very odd-looking mess if anyone had bothered to look. A nearly invisible hawk, morphing into a boy smaller than a toy soldier, while from his legs there grew two much smaller humans.

The Helmacron ship was still dodging and weaving madly, but we were able to hold on. Our small mass meant that our muscles were more than strong enough.

Tobias, with the two of us on his back, went crawling hand over hand toward the engine pods. Meanwhile, of course, the Helmacrons kept up their inevitable bombast.

<We will achieve the greatest victory since the dawn of time as the Yeerk usurpers, humans, and Andalites all come to grovel before us! Yeerk and human and Andalite will compete to see which can abase himself further!>

We reached the engine nacelles. They were warm to the touch but not painfully hot. Tobias helped us down off his back. Marco and I just looked up at him and shook our heads.

"Well, this is definitely it," Marco said. "We have at last achieved Maximum Weirdness. We're the size of pimples, looking up at a bird-turned-boy who looks huge because he's maybe a quarter of an inch tall, as we fly around on the back of a toy-sized spaceship, which we hope to crash by having Cassie turn into a whale the size of a baby mouse, so we can defeat a race of lunatics with brains the size of bacteria. That does it, the votes are in, the Oscar for Absolute Insanity goes to us. Everyone go home. We rule the lunatic world."

Tobias helped to hold me in place. His arm was huge and comforting to me. I don't know, maybe it was the size of a piece of spaghetti. Probably not that big. Marco was right: We were taking up permanent residence in bizarro world.

"Okay," I said to Tobias. "Just hang on till I'm wedged in."

I began to morph. I began to grow. The biggest morph any of us had ever done: the humpback whale.

A real humpback is maybe fifty feet long. Maybe twelve times as long as I am tall, give or take. My baseline now was roughly a sixteenth of an inch. Twelve times a sixteenth of an inch is less than an inch.

But you have to realize that the ratio was for mass, too. In other words, saying "inch-long whale" doesn't really get across the reality. Because in the real world, a humpback might weigh sixty tons.

So as I grew, the Helmacron ship began to feel a weight on its back. A very large weight . . . for them.

I grew and grew and grew, feeling massive, despite the fact that I was no bigger than a goldfish. It hurt a little, being wedged in between the engine nacelles, but at least I wasn't going to fall.

And then, to our utter shock, a hatch opened in the top of the ship. A pair of Helmacron eyes popped up. Then another.

They climbed out and onto the exterior of the ship with us.

<Stop what you are doing and accept your fate as our everlasting slaves!>

<No,> I said. <I'm going to keep morphing and keep getting bigger till I drag this ship down.>

<We are the Helmacrons! We are the rulers of the galaxy! All who oppose us will be utterly annihilated!>

"Oh, shut up," Marco said.

The two Helmacrons gaped at him.

"Just shut up. I mean, shut . . . up. Shut up! You aren't the masters of anything! You're lice, for crying out loud. You're fleas. You couldn't go *mano a mano* with a maggot and hope to win. And that's sad, because a maggot has no *manos*."

Tobias grabbed the two Helmacrons and held them up in the air. Their little legs kicked wildly.

<Bow before us and beg for your lives, abject, insignificant specimens of an inferior species!> the Helmacrons yelped.

"Cassie, morph some more," Marco said.

I resumed morphing and grew still larger. The Helmacron ship wasn't dodging and weaving as well as it had been. It was slowing. It was sagging to the rear.

And it must have been losing altitude as well,

because the reaching, grasping hands were all around us.

Huge fingers like the columns of Greek temples stabbed the air. Nightmare faces the size of Great Lakes were all around us.

The green ray continued to fire, but now the hands and faces were closing in and the little ship was slowing.

"Give it up, you idiots!" Marco raged at the Helmacrons. "Give it up and Cassie will demorph. Surrender so you can get away!"

<We are the Helmacrons! We will never surrender! All will exist only to serve us! All will be our —>

And that's when the really, really, *really* large hand slammed into the side of the ship.

CHAPTER 26

Ш HAMMMMM!
CRRRRRRRUNCH!

Gigantic fingers rose above the edge of the ship. Slowly, slowly, they closed around it.

I could see the swirls of fingerprint. Could see the huge, creek-wide creases and folds in the hand. The ship should have been able to get away, but it was too overburdened. The Helmacrons would not release the blue box, and they would not surrender to us.

My plan was looking like a really bad idea.

"Demorph!" Tobias yelled.

"He's right, demorph!" Marco agreed. "Better the Helmacrons than the Yeerks!"

I started to demorph, shrinking as fast as I could.

Too late!

A thumb the size of Manhattan rose from the far side of the little ship. We were caught!

"I have it!" a monstrous voice bellowed, very close by.

And then, from above and behind the thumb, something that looked exactly like a crescent moon — and was just about that big — came swooping in.

Even to us it seemed to be moving fast. It sliced down and down and down!

FWAPPPP!

Ax's tail blade hit the thumb.

The thumb suddenly disappeared. I heard a world-shattering bellow.

The ship tumbled, out of control, around and around. Tobias let go of the Helmacrons and grabbed the first thing he found to grab. Marco was still so small that he held on with ease, and I was still wedged in place.

A different hand, with more numerous and more slender fingers, reached up and snagged us out of the air.

<I have them, Prince Jake!> Ax cried.

<Then let's haul!> Jake yelled.

<Jake! Where are you?> I yelled in thought-speak, glad to hear his "voice" again.

<I'm about halfway up Ax's leg. I don't know *which* leg.>

<You're safe!>

<Not hardly. Rachel and I are not alone. Visser Three and about twenty Controllers are coming up the leg after us. We've got a very small tiger and a very small grizzly bear here against Visser Three, who has morphed into some kind of bizarre monster!>

<Ax!> I said. <You have to put us on your leg so we can help Jake and Rachel!>

<I do not know which leg they are on,> Ax said tersely.

He was in a full, all-out run now, clutching the Helmacron ship and the blue box in his two weak Andalite hands. One of his fingers was pressing down on me, so I began to demorph to release the pressure.

Tobias crawled back and grabbed me as I shrank far enough to unwedge myself. He pulled me up to sit on his knee like a toddler. Marco was on his other knee. Tobias was leaning back against one of Ax's fingers.

I saw the tops of a row of pinball eyes go marching past, just beyond the finger.

"The Helmacrons!" I hissed, now human again. "They're bailing!"

Tobias twisted his head and caught sight of them, too. He crouched down and motioned

133

Marco to be quiet. Dozens, maybe hundreds, of Helmacrons were abandoning ship, just over in the next space between Andalite fingers.

Tobias was the most visible of us, so he began to demorph back to hawk, making himself much smaller and less obvious to any inquisitive Helmacron.

Marco shook his head and in a voiceless whisper said, "Okay, I admit it. I was wrong. We had not achieved Maximum Weirdness. *Now* we are at Maximum Weirdness."

<I am outrunning my pursuers,> Ax said, <but I am entering areas where I may be seen. I should morph to human. But if I do, the Controllers chasing me may catch up. Also, they would learn that I have a human morph!>

<They know you have a human morph,> Rachel said. <Or at least they could assume it.>

<Rachel's right,> Jake said from his distant location on one of Ax's legs. <You have no choice, Ax. Morph to human.>

<Yes, Prince Jake.>

I was waiting for Jake to tell Ax not to call him "prince." But the next thing I heard from Jake was very different.

<Rachel!> Jake yelled. <It's the Visser! That tentacle! Look out!>

And then Ax began to morph.

<Where should I go?> Ax asked, sounding as

frustrated as I felt. <Tobias! Cassie! Marco! Where should I run when I have formed my human legs?>

I tried to stay calm, but now the shouting between Jake and Rachel told of a fierce, deadly battle taking place amid blue Andalite fur.

Where? Where could we go? What could we do? How could we defeat an enemy small enough to be an ant colony? What weapon could we . . .

And then, with utter simplicity and complete perfection, the answer came to me.

"Tobias," I said. "Tell Ax not to morph to human. We need to fly."

<Fly where?>

"To the zoo. We have to go to The Gardens!"

<But why?>

"To reload," I said grimly. "To reload."

CHAPTER 27

O Most High and Tremendous! A calamity has befallen us! Our own ship has now been captured! But we fear nothing! We are the boldest of the bold, the bravest of the brave! Nothing will stop us as we take control of this vast expanse of huge blue fur, and from that base, launch again our plan to conquer the universe!

— From the log of the Helmacron ship, *Planet Crusher*

I had a plan. A pretty good plan. Just one little problem: We had to stay alive to reach The Gardens.

And that was getting harder real fast.

Ax was morphing from Andalite to northern harrier. That way he could fly and carry the Helmacron ship and the blue box in his talons. And all of us were on him. Marco, Tobias, and I on his fingers. A bunch of Helmacrons on his wrist. Jake and Rachel on one of his legs, running and fighting Visser Three in morph and a bunch of very tiny human-Controllers.

Just one thing. When Ax morphed, not all his body parts stayed in the same locations. Each morph is different. I don't know why — they just are. And now, as Ax's body began to melt and shrink and run together, unfortunate things were happening.

The hand we were on was ceasing to exist.

It was like we were standing on molasses. The skin beneath us and around us melted slowly together. It ran beneath our feet, a slow-moving sludgy river. The gigantic finger to our left and the equally gigantic finger to our right were running together. The molasses skin filled the gap between, raising us higher relative to the fingers. But lower, too, because the whole time Ax was shrinking.

Suddenly we seemed to be moving on a swift conveyer belt that went off the edge of the world. It was like we were on a conveyer belt that became an escalator that then got steeper and steeper!

"Look out!" Marco cried.

<Morph to birds!> Tobias shouted as he flapped his wings and went airborne.

I was slipping, sliding on my belly, grabbing frantically at slick, moving, flowing skin. Beneath me a fall of miles!

Then . . . a handhold!

My fingers grabbed. Bare millimeters to grasp, but the ledge I held to was growing deeper. My wildly swinging feet found another crack. I clung to a shifting, melting, slithering cliff side!

The angle got worse still. I was upside down! And yet with my insignificant mass, I found I could hold on to the widening cracks.

Marco was dangling not far away, also digging frantic hands and blind feet into cracks in the cliff.

We would have fallen. But for the fact that gigantic feather patterns were appearing across the melting skin. The patterns traveled over the skin like the cracks on a thawing frozen lake. The patterns had just a bit of depth. Just enough for a sixteenth-of-an-inch-tall creature to grip.

Then, between Marco and me, an explosion! The "ground" erupted as the shallow feather pattern suddenly became fully three-dimensional.

SPRRROOOOOOT!

A feather sprouted between us, sweeping us up into its heights. Gray and white vanes grew out of the central shaft, thickening and stiffening till they felt like large bamboo sticks.

The feather lay back then, closely packed with feathers above and below and all around us.

At this point we were almost horizontal again. It was a gentle slope down the feather shaft to the "ground." I felt a slow, steady, up-and-down motion, though that changed the slope from down to up and back again.

"We're on a wing," Marco said.

Tobias came swooping in and landed hard. <You're on a wing feather,> he said, gasping and panting. <I can't fly. Too much turbulence! And we have trouble!>

"Trouble?" Marco said, mocking. "Trouble? What makes you say we have trouble? Everything seems fine to me. Perfectly fine. I have never been better."

Tobias didn't laugh. <Somehow we all ended up on the same wing. One of Ax's legs must have melded with his hand to make this wing. Jake and Rachel are just half an inch away. The Yeerks are coming on fast, and the Helmacrons are forming into what looks like an army about a quarter of an inch over that way.>

"See? I told you everything was fine."

"Marco, we have to morph. We can't let the Yeerks see us as humans," I said.

Moments later, a gorilla and a wolf resided in the weird forest of feathers. We trotted down the feather to the "ground," the dimpled bird flesh beneath us. And just in time.

A tiger and a grizzly bear came racing toward us, staggering through the slanted quills. Since Jake and Rachel had been shrunk while in morph, they, too, were a sixteenth of an inch tall.

Jake's tiger face was bloody. He was panting, but not beaten yet.

<Good to see you guys,> he said.

<Where are the Yeerks?> Tobias asked.

<Oh, they'll be here pretty quick. The Visser is in some weird morph. Lots of bladed tentacles. Like a Hork-Bajir on steroids. Plus there's a bunch of very scared human-Controllers.>

<I'm tired of running,> Rachel said. <Let's just do this right here.>

Jake and Rachel joined us, shoulder to shoulder. A huge, lumbering bear, a lithe tiger, a powerful gorilla, and me, a wolf with senses that could smell and hear and almost taste the approaching Yeerks.

I was so focused on the Yeerks, I almost didn't hear the other sound.

But then the Visser's monstrous morph came rushing from the feather forest. It was like a blood-orange Medusa's head, each hair snake carrying a scythe. Crowding in behind him were a bunch of very nervous-looking human-Controllers, including Chapman.

Visser Three came to a stop. We stood facing him.

I saw none of the Visser's usual cool arrogance. <Strange place to meet for our final battle, Andalites,> he said. <But battle we must.>

That was pretty calm for him. I think maybe the fact that he was the size of a dandruff flake depressed him.

We faced off, Yeerk versus human, although the Yeerks still believed us to be Andalites.

And then, from the feathers to our right, there appeared dozens of four-legged, flat-headed, BB-eyed creatures.

<Hah! All our pitiful foes gathered together! All the better to quake in terror before Helmacron might! Surrender and live out your pitiful lives as our slaves, or fight us and die as weaklings!>

For a long, frozen moment, no one moved.

Twisting his tentacles aside to reveal a hideous face, the Visser looked at us. <I don't know about you, Andalites,> he said, <but these creatures are really, really, *really* annoying me.>

Now, I know it's not possible for a tiger to grin, but I swear Jake did.

And for the first and probably last time in history, humans and Yeerks turned as one to face a common enemy.

Unfortunately, or fortunately, the truce didn't last long. Because just then Ax announced, <We are over The Gardens.>

I gave him quick thought-speak directions and yelled to the others. <We have to get off this bird!>

<What?> Jake demanded.

<We have to jump,> I said. <We have to jump off Ax.>

<Excuse me?> Rachel said. <We're like a billion miles up!>

<Just trust me,> I said. <Go to the end of a feather and get ready to jump!>

CHAPTER 28

I ran. They followed. We left the Yeerks to face the Helmacrons, who, naturally, were yammering happily about us. <Fleeing like quivering cowards before the very flower of Helmacron might!>

<I don't like running away,> Rachel growled. But she followed me as we hauled along a slanted feather shaft.

It was a long run, but suddenly we could feel a powerful wind blowing over us. Wind like a hurricane.

<Ax! Are we there?> I cried.

<One moment . . . Prepare yourselves . . .>

<Jake, Rachel, everyone,> I said, <when Ax says jump, leap off the edge of the feather. We're

143

too small to get hurt falling. Besides, we'll have a soft landing. As soon as he —>

Suddenly, the Visser's monstrous morph was rushing toward us. <I changed my mind,> he said. <I think I'd rather kill *you*!>

<NOW!> Ax yelled.

We jumped. Each to the limits of his abilities. My wolf body jumped pretty well. And then I was falling. Falling forever, with a grizzly bear not so far above me.

Beyond the bear and the tiger, I saw a shocking sight. The Visser had followed us! His octopuslike morph was falling, legs flailing. And behind him, like so many suicidal jumpers, came a dozen or more human-Controllers.

Far above, at the limits of my vision, I saw a lemming rush of Helmacrons. But because Ax was moving slightly, we were all spread out across the sky. Us, then the Yeerks, then the Helmacrons.

We fell and fell and . . .

POOMP!

. . . landed.

We landed in rough fur. I tumbled between a pair of hairs and fell some more. In my wolf morph I couldn't grab hold with anything but my powerful teeth. So that's just what I did. I clamped my teeth around a stiff, springy hair.

Once I saw that Rachel, Jake, and Marco were

all safe on the skin floor beneath us, I let go and dropped.

I landed on all fours. And instantly I began to demorph.

<You going to tell us what this is all about?> Jake demanded, none too gently.

<I'm not totally sure,> I admitted. <But something occurred to me: When the Hel-macrons shrank us, they also shrank all the DNA inside us. All the morphs were reduced to that same scale, right?>

<So?> Marco asked.

<Well, it occurred to me that new DNA, newly *acquired* DNA, might not be shrunk.>

Jake was already halfway to human. <Hey! You're saying that —> His thought-speak ceased as he made the transition out of morph.

I was almost fully human, standing crouched beneath a huge hair. "Yes," I said. "At least, I hope. We should be able to acquire this animal we're on and morph it. Full size!"

I dropped to my knees and pressed my hands against the flesh. But before I could focus, some-thing hideous bounded wildly into the middle of our group.

"Aaaahhhh!" I screamed and leaped back.

Everyone fell back, shocked and horrified be-fore the armored, inhuman creature.

The flea . . . because that's what it was, a

flea . . . didn't look at us with its tiny black ball-bearing eyes. Its eyes didn't exactly focus. And we'd have been of no interest, anyway.

But even knowing that, the sight of a flea the size of a human was terrifying. They are vile-looking little monsters. I know. I've been one.

The flea seemed to consider whether it should do something. Decided not to. And fired its spring-loaded legs.

It blew up and out of sight with a speed that was almost comical.

"Let's get big before we run into any more of them," Rachel said. "I don't like this forest. Lions and tigers and fleas. Oh my."

I dropped to my knees again and focused on the animal beneath us. The others did the same.

"Hey, what are we acquiring?" Jake asked.

"The one animal in the world that is specially designed to see, attack, and destroy creatures like the Helmacrons," I said grimly.

"And that animal is . . ."

"Anteater," I said.

CHAPTER 29

"Let's give it a try," Jake said. "Let's get big!"

I have morphed many times and many animals. But I don't ever remember such a satisfying feeling. I wanted to be big again. I wanted to get back to a world where fleas and mites were . . . well, fleas and mites.

I was growing swiftly, my human features already melted and distorted, as the Visser burst into view through the fur.

He gaped up at us as we grew.

<Of course!> he said.

But I couldn't worry about him right then because I was growing at a shocking, wonderful rate. Up, up through the fur! Up till my head was clear of the anteater's back. Up and up till Tobias flying past seemed small.

Up and up till a much larger Ax in harrier morph seemed no bigger than a 747.

Up till I could see the others, all rising from the fur like hot air balloons ascending from a jungle.

The anteater gave a sudden shake, having felt us, and we tumbled to the ground. But it was wonderful. When we hit the dirt it was just dirt.

We were getting big again!

As you'd expect, the anteater I was becoming had good eyes, at least for small details. I could see Ax resting. I could see Tobias on his shoulder. And I could see the Helmacron ship with the blue box still attached, lying in the dirt with Ax's harrier talon wrapped protectively around it.

An anteater is a funny-looking animal. From the end of its bushy, feather-duster tail to the tip of its absurdly long, pointed head, it was maybe four or four and a half feet long. It stood as tall as a grown man's knees. Not a huge animal. But wonderfully big to all of us.

I looked out through keen, anteater eyes and saw a field of vision half-filled by the furred tube that was its mouth. It seemed to stretch out forever.

But even though the giant anteater is comical, it is not helpless. I was resting most of my weight on my hind legs. I balanced on my front knuckles, the better to keep my wickedly curved scythe claws safe and sharp.

I felt the anteater instincts bubbling up beneath my own human consciousness. I braced myself for some extreme fight-or-flight reaction. But the anteater was a calm, lethargic sort of creature. Later I found out they have one of the lowest body temperatures of any land mammal. They're known to sleep as much as fifteen hours a day.

But this was not a stupid animal. I had excellent hearing and an excellent sense of smell.

And I could quite clearly see the rushing groups of Helmacrons and human-Controllers on the ground.

I was in such control of my more obvious instincts that I didn't really even think about what happened next.

Flit!

My tongue shot out an amazing two feet! It slapped a gaggle of Helmacrons, bathed them in sticky spit, snagged them with the tiny barbs of the anteater tongue, and snapped them back into my mouth before I knew what I'd done.

<Go, Cassie!> Marco said.

I felt something in my mouth, something kind of like teeth, only not, begin to chew . . .

<No!> I yelled, freezing my jaw muscles.

Then, to my utter astonishment, I heard from deep inside my own mouth, <Surrender now and we may spare you the eternal torment you have earned!>

I shot my tongue back out, and with a great effort of will, kept it there, sticking out, lying flat on the dirt. Stuck to my tongue were a couple of dozen Helmacrons.

<You know, I really don't want to have to kill you,> I said.

<Surrender and grovel before us!>

I heard another thought-speak voice. Lower and more sinister. <Sentimental Andalite fool,> Visser Three said. He had copied our trick. He had also morphed the anteater. <You can't kill a Helmacron. They're a fungible species. Kill one and its mind, if you can call it a mind, is absorbed into another. They *never* die. Even when they're dead, they're not dead. But when it comes to Andalites . . .>

Flit!

His tongue shot out and snagged not an ant, but a very small bird that had been flying by.

<Aaahhhh!> Tobias cried.

<Tobias!> Rachel screamed.

The Visser stopped his tongue, holding a stuck and helpless Tobias a millimeter from disappearing into his tubular jaw.

<Now we shall talk,> Visser Three sneered.

Like lightning, Ax leaped. Like lightning, his tail blade came down and stopped, quivering, pressed against the Visser's anteater throat.

<*Now* we shall talk,> Ax said.

CHAPTER 30

We worked out a deal.

Rachel and Jake lapped up the Helmacrons and held them hostage. It was a relief to know that Helmacrons were basically unkillable. Well, mostly a relief. In any case, they were stuck.

Marco and I demorphed back to our tiny human selves. We did it out of sight of Visser Three, of course. And then we boarded the Helmacron ship. We found some of the pathetically easy-to-intimidate males and had them help us work the Helmacron shrinking ray.

We unshrank Visser Three and Tobias while Ax stood guarding the Visser, the Helmacron ship, and the blue box, tail blade twitching.

We unshrank the human-Controllers and gave the Yeerks safe passage to leave. They weren't about to argue. After all, we were in control of the shrinking ray.

Visser Three decided maybe the conquest of Earth would work better if he was bigger than a semicolon.

When the Yeerks were gone, Rachel and Jake scraped the Helmacrons off their tongues and demorphed to human. We unshrank them.

Finally, we set the thing on automatic and Marco and I ran outside to stand in the beam.

But not before we had a good, long talk with some of the Helmacron males.

"You guys need a males' liberation movement," Marco told them. "Why should you put up with being treated like second-class Helmacrons?"

And many of the males agreed. <We could crush the females beneath our feet! Long would they wail and bemoan their fate as we assumed our places as the rightful rulers of all Helmacrons! We would then proceed with our just and righteous plans to conquer all the galaxy! Then all would grovel before us and . . .>

Well, you know the rest.

"About time to head on home, huh?" Jake asked me.

I nodded. "Yeah. As it is, I'm probably grounded."

"Oh. I hope not. I was, uh . . . I don't know, I was thinking maybe of heading down to the beach tomorrow. You know, if the weather's nice."

Rachel batted her eyes at me and gave me an "I told you so" look. Then, just to be obnoxious, she said, "Oh, I don't know, Jake, I don't think Cassie really likes the beach all that —"

"I love the beach," I said, shooting her a death look. "And if I don't get grounded, I'd love to go with you, Jake."

Jake blushed, waiting for Marco to give him grief. But Marco just shook his head in a parody of sadness. "Fine, Cassie. Run back to Jake now that you're all big again. I guess that's the end of our plan to populate the world with a new race of tiny people."

The Helmacron ship powered up and rose toward the night sky. And receding in the distance, we heard the thought-speak voices.

<All females will now grovel before our tremendous power! You will worship us as your true masters! It is the male Helmacron who shall make all tremble!>

<Never will females be anything but absolute

rulers over all males! We shall dominate the entire universe, but we'll start with you!>

We headed home, leaving the Helmacrons, female and male, to work things out sensibly among themselves. Knowing, with absolute certainty, that there was no chance they would.

I stopped breathing. Hork-Bajir were every-where. Everywhere!

This wouldn't be a fight. This would be a slaughter.

Then, at the center door, *he* appeared.

<Well, well, well. Here aboard my own ship. How nice of you to come around to see me. Can I offer you anything? Something to drink? To eat? Or maybe just a quick death?>

The Visser laughed. He had reason to laugh. Three doors open and filled with Dracon-armed Hork-Bajir.

<Give the word, Jake,> Rachel whispered. <Give the word and I swear I can at least get *him*.>

Three doors? Wasn't there a fourth door? And why wasn't it open?

<Ax!> I said urgently. <I don't want to turn around and look, but is there a fourth door?>

Ax swiveled one stalk eye. <Yes! It must lead to the exterior of the ship. But there is a control pad protecting the emergency manual release. It is undoubtedly coded. It would take me hours to find the security code.>

Of course. And Visser Three knew that. But maybe this wasn't a case for subtlety. I flexed my canned ham fist. <Jake! There's another door behind us. A keypad. Maybe I can break it open.>

<And get fried before you twitch,> Jake pointed out.

<No. The Yeerks will not fire weapons in here. Not with those canisters,> Ax said. <They are obviously valuable specimens.>

Jake reached a very fast decision. <Rachel. Next word Visser Three says, you slam the nearest canister. Marco, The keypad. Ax, back Marco up. Tobias, Cassie, and me, straight at Visser Three, a feint.>

I was getting ready to make a lame pun about "feint" and "faint" when the Visser spoke.

<Surrender now and —>

Before he could get to his fourth word, Rachel struck! A mountain of grizzly slammed hard into the nearest cylinder.

WHAM!

Nothing!

Too late, I'd already spun around and bounded toward the keypad.

<KILL THEM!> Visser Three screamed.

"*Tseeeeer*!" Tobias screamed.

"Hraawwwrrr!" Rachel bellowed. She slammed all her weight this time, all her strength.

Crack!

A single crack, a small, pathetic crack, appeared in the cylinder wall. The mist began to seep out.

Jake, Cassie, and Tobias attacked. No other option now.

I saw a flash of orange and black leaping straight at Visser Three. No less than half a dozen Hork-Bajir enveloped him, blades flashing.

I saw the keypad. I drew back my pile-driver arm and slammed it with all my might. It crumpled like a tin can.

<Rip away the metal!> Ax yelled, even as he used his reversed stalk eyes to aim a sonic-boom tail snap at a rushing Hork-Bajir.

Rachel withdrew, backed up a dozen feet, and ran all-out, full-speed, on all fours at the cylinder. A small army of Hork-Bajir leaped after her.

Just then, I saw Cassie flying through the air. Not a leap. She'd been thrown, bloodied and broken.

Tobias was in the air, harassing Visser Three, aiming for his vulnerable stalk eyes.

WHAM!

Rachel hit the cylinder. A flailing mob of Hork-Bajir literally covered her.

And then the cylinder shattered.

CRASH! It fell in pieces.

Whoosh! The mist inside billowed out. Hork-Bajir screamed and tried to back away. But too late! The clouds of mist caught them, freezing any body part it touched.

Not freezing, as in it made them cold. Freezing, as in solid. Like stone gargoyles. I saw one puzzled Hork-Bajir gape in horror as his left leg simply broke off and lay on the deck like a piece of a statue.

The mist hit Rachel, too. But she had a thick coat of fur. The fur froze and shattered off like thousands of brittle needles.

I ripped away the loose metal of the keypad.

<Squeeze that handle!> Ax ordered.

I squeezed.

Too late, Visser Three saw his mistake. <Bridge!> he roared. <Bridge, get us up! Get us up!>

The outer hull door began to slide. It opened onto empty whiteness.

<Jake! Cassie! Everyone! Door open! Bail!> I yelled.

The freezing mist was swirling around the

floor now, forcing the Visser to back up. But that didn't mean he wouldn't send his troops into it.

<After them! After them!>

Hork-Bajir plowed through the mist and found themselves on frozen feet. Feet with toes that broke off, with ankles that snapped.

Jake coiled his tiger muscles and took the mist at a leap. Tobias was first out the door. Cassie lay unconscious in a heap, with mist advancing on her.

Without hesitation, Rachel walked into the mist and lifted Cassie's wolf body with her teeth. The grizzly's left foot stayed where it had frozen. Rachel staggered to the door on a stump.

One by one, we tumbled out of the door and into emptiness.

Before the Animorphs...

Three aliens battled together...

In the ultimate fight for freedom...

Read their story.
So much you do not know.

<It's Here>

ANIMORPHS

1999 Wall Calendar

- Illustrated by the Animorphs cover artist.
- Features a different Animorph each month.
- Includes all the morphs, vital stats, plus—secret messages from the Animorphs!

Mind-blowing Cover that Changes Before Your Eyes!

Watch Animorphs on Television this Fall!